Frances Freeling Broderip

Tales of the Toys

Told by themselves

Frances Freeling Broderip

Tales of the Toys
Told by themselves

ISBN/EAN: 9783337074876

Printed in Europe, USA, Canada, Australia, Japan

Cover: Foto ©Andreas Hilbeck / pixelio.de

More available books at **www.hansebooks.com**

HURRAH! WE ARE GOING TO SANDBAY.

TALES OF THE TOYS,

Told by Themselves.

by

FRANCES FREELING BRODERIP.

AUTHOR OF "MY GRANDMOTHER'S BUDGET," "MERRY SONGS FOR LITTLE
VOICES," "MAMMA'S MORNING GOSSIPS," ETC.

With Illustrations by Tom Hood.

LONDON:

GRIFFITH AND FARRAN,

(Successors to Newbery and Harris,)

CORNER OF ST. PAUL'S CHURCHYARD

CONTENTS.

CHAPTER I.

CHAPTER II.

CHAPTER III.

CHAPTER IV.

TALES OF THE TOYS.

CHAPTER I.—INTRODUCTORY.

THE TURNING OUT OF THE TOY CUPBOARD.

"HURRAH! We are going to have such a jolly holiday!" shouted Frank, suddenly bursting out of his imprisonment in the slate closet, to the great disturbance of his sisters, who were peaceably occupied with their lessons.

"Frank," said Miss Watson, "I must really at last report you to your Papa. I do not like to trouble him if I can help it, but I am afraid you will oblige me to do so. I desired you not to leave the book closet until you had made up your mind to sit straight on your chair, and go through the multiplication table properly."

"We're to go to Sandbay for a month!"

shouted Frank, capering about and clapping his hands.

"To Sandbay, Frank! oh, how charming!" cried Celia and Florry, with one voice.

"We shall be able to collect so many shells, and perhaps to get some anemones!" said Celia.

"I shall make such gardens and ovens in the sand!" cried Florry, opening her blue eyes as wide as possible. "I wonder what has become of my spade?"

"I'll leave Pa no peace till he takes me out for a sail," said Frank, whose antics had not yet subsided.

"I think you have all gone suddenly mad!" said Miss Watson. "Celia, I am surprised at *you!* I have ceased to hope for quiet manners from Frank, and Florry is so little, she scarcely knows better; but your giddiness is not usual."

"I beg your pardon, Miss Watson," replied Celia, demurely; "only it was so nice to think of going to the Sea."

"But I don't understand the matter now," said poor Miss Watson, looking very mystified; "you knew nothing about this at breakfast, Frank, and how your companionship with the

books and slates in the cupboard has enlightened
you now, I don't know, nor can I give even a
remote guess!"

" Why, the store cupboard in the dining room
is next to the book closet," replied Frank, eagerly,
" and just now, when I had got my hand on the
lock of the door to come out and tell you I had
had enough of solitary imprisoning, I heard
Mamma come into the store cupboard (for some
jam, I daresay!) and she said out loud to some-
body, ' I mean to take the children for a month
to Sandbay this summer!' That's what made me
rush out to tell the girls the good news!"

" Well, Frank, I never believed you guilty of
the meanness of listening before," said Miss
Watson, rather severely.

" I didn't listen," said Frank, rather sulkily.

" You can hear very plainly in the book closet,
Miss Watson," said Celia. " When I have put
away the books sometimes, I have heard Ellen
laying the luncheon in the dining room from the
store cupboard door being left open. I am sure
we should not listen on purpose, and I don't
think Frank could help hearing it, if Mamma
spoke distinctly."

"It's very nice of you, Celia, to be always so ready to excuse your brother," said Miss Watson, "and I *do* believe Frank above such mean, dishonest habits as that; and so I suppose I must overlook his boisterous conduct this once, as the news he heard by accident seems so exciting to you all."

"Oh, Miss Watson, don't you like the sea too?" enquired little Florry; "it's so nice to stand on a heap of sand and let the waves come round you."

"Well, Florry," replied Miss Watson, smiling, "there are many more pleasant things at the seaside than getting your feet wet through; but I suppose *you* like letting the waves chase you!"

"Then there is the bathing," said Celia, delightedly; "I do so love a dip in the cool, green salt water, and the dancing about in it, and waiting for a great wave to come over one!"

"Girls ought to learn to swim!" said Frank, very sententiously. "Suppose a big wave carried you out of your depth, and no one was near to fetch you out again but the old Molly of a bathing woman!"

"I have not the least doubt in the world,"

said Miss Watson, "that you will all enjoy your trip to Sandbay very much. But I think people should *earn* their holiday before they have it, or even waste much time beforehand in planning how to spend it. We shall get no lessons at all this morning if we are to be hindered like this, and the consequence will be, Frank, that as so often is the case, you will spend your playtime in going over them again."

"Suppose we all settle down steadily," suggested sensible Celia, "and put the thoughts of the sea out of our minds till we have done. Look, Miss Watson, it only wants a quarter to one, and we have finished all but our copies!"

"There's the 'vexation' to be got through first, by me at any rate," said Frank, with a rueful air. "I wish the man who invented it had all the 'three times' from one to twelve printed on him with a cat-o'-nine tails, every time a fellow is forced to go through it!"

"When you are a rich old merchant in the City, Frank," replied Miss Watson, smiling," you will find the 'vexation' a pleasure, as you add up your pounds and shillings, or calculate the value of your cargoes!"

"I wonder if Sir Walter Raleigh bothered his head with all this rubbish," growled Frank. "I daresay he counted up his ingots on his fingers. Such a leader as he was never wasted his time and trouble on the bothering old multiplication tables, *I* know."

"Raleigh was a scholar and a poet too, Frank," replied Miss Watson; "you could hardly have chosen a worse example of your theory. He was an Oriel College man, and wrote a history of the world during his captivity in the Tower. He employed his imprisonment better than you have done, you see!"

"I have finished my copy, Miss Watson," said Celia, "may I go now, please? I have nothing more to do until the afternoon."

"Yes, Celia; but, Florry, how carelessly you have written yours.! I am afraid the thoughts of going to the sea have bewildered your little head so, that your fingers have travelled along without any guidance, like runaway horses with the coachman fast asleep!"

Florry blushed and hung her head over the ill-written book, and was silent, for she knew that she had been thinking more of the pleasure before her, and musing where her wooden spade could be, than of her lessons; I am afraid that morning set a mark of "Careless!" in both Frank's and her score. However, school time ended at last, and off with a shout went Frank to hear all about the plans from Celia, for he had no doubt she had been talking the matter over with Mamma. Miss Watson was putting on her bonnet and mantle in order to return home for the usual weekly half holiday, when Mrs. Spenser entered the room.

"I find, Miss Watson," said she, smiling, "that Frank's long ears have managed to catch what Mr. Spenser and I have been arranging for the summer holidays. The house is so very dirty and worn now, after our long residence in it, that we find it will be best to set about a thorough course of paint, paper, and white-wash, so that I have resolved to give the children a month at Sandbay during these holidays, which will do them all a great deal of good, I think."

"I hope it will, indeed," replied Miss Watson; "and I am sure you will find it more agreeable to leave the house in possession of the workmen; all painting and papering is so unpleasant to endure."

"Yes, indeed," said Mrs. Spenser, "I have a great horror of the whole operation; and, besides, Mr. Spenser thinks it will be more thoroughly done, if everything is packed away, and we are all out of the house. It will be very pleasant to be away from the heat of town, and with plenty of sea breezes to freshen up the children. Celia, I think, is looking rather delicate."

"A little sea wind, and a few rambles on the shore, will soon bring back her rosy cheeks," replied Miss Watson, shaking hands with Mrs. Spenser, as she took her leave. "I hope you will all be very much the better for the change."

For the rest of the next week—the last but one before the holidays began—Binswood Villa was a scene of endless bustle and confusion. The children enjoyed it all immensely, and rejoiced secretly at the little interruptions to the usual routine of their daily lessons, which were now taken in "pic-nic fashion," as Celia declared. For after the dining-room was cleared of its furniture, the schoolroom was obliged to be used for luncheon and dinner. And at last, joy of joys, the schoolroom itself had to be partially given up, and the weather being very warm and dry, the last few days' school was held in the arbour in the garden. The children enjoyed the remove greatly; but Frank declared that it was a sore trial to Miss Watson, for she had earwigs up her sleeve and snails on her gown!

"I am too fond of a garden, Frank, to mind even these mishaps," said Miss Watson, laughing; "and as they have not yet fallen to my share, I won't fear them beforehand. I think all the garden inhabitants recognise *you* for their lawful prey, for I can see a little money-spinner spider making a tour of your collar now!"

Then there was all the packing to be done. Mamma very wisely got over her share of the business during the quiet hours when the young folks were at school, and, therefore, managed to get everything stowed away in tolerable order. And she found out the wisdom of her plan soon enough, for the confusion and trouble that reigned during the three days' holiday before they left, nearly drove poor Nurse out of her senses. But at last even all these worries were happily got over, and Celia's treasures safely put away, Frank's bat and ball and cricket-shoes hunted up, and Florry's missing wooden spade found behind the clock-case.

Mrs. Spenser and the Nurse had the worst part of the business even now, in arranging and packing all the frocks and pinafores, socks and jackets in small compass for their long visit. Young folks are very apt not to think of all these things, and seem to imagine that hats and caps, gloves and shoes grow on the bushes, and are produced by rain and sunshine, like the garments of the flowers! Most mothers and nurses could tell a very different tale; and could, if they pleased, prove, that if little girls were as idly managed as the doll family are, life would not be so easy or quite so pleasant, to the juveniles at least.

At last the happy day of the journey arrived, and the Spensers, with all their luggage, were safely crammed into a couple of cabs, and borne off to the railway station on their way to Sand-bay. Little Florry persisted in carrying her precious wooden spade, for fear it should be left behind, a proceeding that resulted in its being left in the refreshment-room at Hembery station, and only regained at the risk of Frank's being left behind; and it was finally forgotten in the carriage when they changed at Dawlish junction, its little tired owner being carried fast asleep in Nurse's arms. And so before Papa left them all comfortably settled in their airy lodgings at Sandbay, he was obliged to take his tearful little girl to the one toy-shop and buy her a new one.

"Which you gained by, Florry," remarked Frank; "for Pa gave you a bucket into the bargain; so now you can make ovens enough to bake all the rolls in Sandbay!"

And then, like a good-natured brother as he was, he printed Florry's name in great capital letters on her spade, with the name of the house they lived in, so that when she left it behind on the sands, there was a chance of its being brought back again. And Celia and her mother rambled about by the edge of the sea, and collected shells and sea-weed, or took long walks through the pretty country round Sandbay, till the rosy cheeks Miss Watson prophesied became quite Celia's usual look.

Meanwhile, Mr. Spenser having seen the little colony comfortably established, returned back to town, for he was going to stay with a sister who lived near his own house, in order to keep an occasional watch over the workmen. And so the town villa, which a few hours before had been the scene of such confusion and bustle,— such noisy voices and pattering feet,—was left empty to the echoes and the dust which now had time to settle peaceably over the bare boards and dingy windows. An old charwoman had the charge of it, and was to sleep in the kitchen; but as the workmen were not to come till the day after, she contented herself with merely sweeping down the house in the afternoon, ready for the whitewashers next day; and then, locking all up safe, with old Growler, the dog, inside, she set off, after an early cup of tea, to get in her provisions for the next day.

It was, indeed, a change! The bed-rooms had lost their nice white little beds and curtains; the drawing-room was a dusty desert, with no piano and no work-tables; while the kitchen yawned like a gloomy cavern, stripped of its bright tins and cheerful dishes. And the dusky shades of evening fell and wrapped it in still darker shadows, while the distant roar and din of the streets seemed to sound quite far off. So then the crickets, who felt sure something unusual must be the matter, chirped, and made enquiries of each other, in the most noisy manner; while the mice, quite enraptured with the quiet and vacancy, came out and had regular pic-nic parties all over the house.

The furniture and packages had all been stowed away in one large room at the top of the house, which had then been securely locked and fastened. But one nook had been neglected in the midst of all the bustle. Busy as she had been with preparing the summer clothes, putting away all the winter ones, and setting aside all in her own particular domain, Nurse had utterly overlooked the old toy cupboard! It is true it was now seldom used; for even Florry cared little for the broken and discarded toys it contained, and so it was not to be wondered at that the old store of rubbish had not been remembered. Some officious person had unlatched the door and left it ajar, and a good blast of wind in the afternoon, when old Mrs.

Davis set the window open first, had pushed it quite back, though she had not observed the fact when she closed the nursery windows before she left. On the floor lay a heap of old leaden tea-things, mixed up with some of the inhabitants of a battered Noah's Ark which lay empty on its side on the top shelf. Several old marbles were nestled cosily up in an old toy kitchen which had been turned upside down to receive them. A humming-top, whose key had departed, lay side by side with a shuttlecock that had been shorn of half its feathers. The skipping-rope had become hopelessly entangled with the tail of the kite; the hoop had hung itself round the neck of a very ancient rocking-horse, whose mane and tail had long disappeared; to add to its mis-fortunes the poor animal now lacked the whole of one leg, and part of another, and being past mending, it had not seen daylight for a long while. A doll, with one arm, and whose bland, faded face had lost all expression with her missing eyes, presided in a solemn manner over the whole. The shelf above was empty, with one exception, for on it lay a very large ball, made of leather in many pieces, carefully joined together.   Why it had been placed in the old toy cupboard was a mystery, for it seemed nearly new from the brightness of its colours and the full roundness of its form.   That it was gifted with more strength and vitality than its companions was evident enough, for it gave a violent roll on the shelf, and then bounded suddenly down into the midst of its companions.

"And so *we've* got a holiday at last," said the Ball, with a lively frisk as he spoke.

"Oh! don't be so rough," faintly shrieked the Doll; "you have almost taken away all the little breath I had left!"

"I'll fan you with the greatest pleasure!" said the Kite, eagerly, "or at least, I'll try to do so, for I have stood here so long, that I am quite stiff, but I'll do my best!"

And so he vigorously flapped backwards and forwards, till all the dust was set in motion that had rested quiet so long.   So that at last, the Rocking-horse even was roused from his long slumber, and hobbled out of the corner on his lame legs.

"How very pleasant!" exclaimed the Ball, hopping about with the greatest agility; "I declare it is quite worth while living in retirement for a while, if only to enjoy life once more when we come back to it again. How's the Doll now?" enquired he, politely, bounding towards her.

"Better I hope," puffed the Kite; "but you know this cupboard has been stifling for a long while, and so now the first breeze of fresh air is almost too much for us all."

"Speak for yourself," snapped the Shuttle-cock, very peevishly; "you have fanned out my last feather, and what I'm to do now I can't think; I'm nothing but cork and leather!"

"We are none of us much to be boasted of," remarked the old leaden Teapot; "I'm sure I have been battered and dinted till I've no shape left. But one gets used in time to being trodden on."

"Yes, indeed, and to get one's horns and legs snapped off," chimed in an eager lilac wooden Cow, who certainly had lost most of her members, "over and above parting with your relations. My twin brother was destroyed ages ago, and so was the scarlet cat's, and there's not even one elephant left in the ark, nor a camel, nor a canary, nor a ladybird, nor a bear."

"Oh! never mind your elephants and lady-birds," interrupted the Ball, irreverently; " we shall waste all our time in this arguing and quarrelling!"

"It's easy for you to talk, young man," remarked the Shuttlecock, sarcastically; "*you* have never been into the battle of life, or lost all your feathers."

" This is very stupid work," said the Skipping-rope, coiling about and trying to disentangle herself from the Kite, a proceeding that resulted in one of her handles coming off, and the Kite being shorn of the tassel at the end of his tail.

"Well, what *are* we to do with ourselves," asked the Rocking-Horse, "we are not all of us quite so lively as you, my friend Ball. To us a holiday conveys the idea of *rest*, not restlessness."

" Then I should think holidays were super-fluous things to you!" muttered the Ball, as he took an extra roll out into the room; "but what are we to do, then?"

"Tell stories," suggested the Doll, and the Rocking-Horse and Kite seconded the motion. The Ball bounded about very impatiently, and

proposed a game of play, but he was outvoted,
and the first motion was carried.   But the noise
of the argument had awakened the Humming-
top, and he began to buzz and hum in such a
drony, drowsy fashion, that in sheer terror and
dread, the Ball threw himself gallantly into the
gap, and promised to tell the first story himself,
on condition that he should be allowed to roll
softly about the room for the rest of the evening.
This was very willingly agreed to, and all the
party being comfortably arranged, the Doll having taken care to ensure the services of the Kite,
the Ball begun his proffe d story in the follow-
ing manner.

CHAPTER II.

"IF I were not of a very lively character," remarked the Ball, "I
should feel rather shy at making my
first appearance as a story teller.   But you know
all people of my giddy habits are not much given
to serious consideration.   We make a bold spring
and bound down into the middle of a matter, while
all the graver folks are nervously trembling on
the very brink.   And so, instead of beginning
at the very first chapter of my story, and telling
you that I first grew on an animal's back as
skin, and was then turned into leather, I will
skip the dry part of my history, and begin with
some of my later impressions."

"Now," said the Humming-top, gravely, "I
think I must rather protest against this summary
way of disposing of some of the most interesting

facts respecting your origin. I should like to
know a little more about you, my dear friend.
Pray indulge us with all the particulars of your
early years: your first recollections."

"I had thought," said the Ball, modestly,
"that all these minute facts could hardly be very
interesting, and I have a great fear of tiring out
your attention, and of being called *prosy*," added
he, slily.

"That is impossible," answered the Humming-top, in a pompous manner; "let me beg
of you to relieve our curiosity. I am sure I may
speak for all the rest of our friends," said he,
with a very solemn bow to each member of the
party. The Toys, only too ready to enjoy the
least variation of their long retired life, eagerly
agreed, and the Ball resumed his story:—

"I am afraid I am not very clever at giving
accurate descriptions of things in which I don't
take much interest, and as you may suppose my
real life only begun when all my several portions
were collected together. I am composed, as you
see, of several sections, each of the same size and
shape, but all varying in colour and material.
This quarter of me is composed of two portions

of a pale, tawny leather; and this grew on the back of a fine robust young lamb, who frisked away his brief life on a sunny pasture in Denmark. He formed one of the members of a huge flock of sheep, belonging to a well-to-do farmer, whose riches in herds of cattle and flocks of sheep were accumulating for the dowry of his only child Mari. She was the best dowered maiden for fifty miles round, and though young in her teens, made the yellowest butter and firmest cheese for three villages round. Her father was a thrifty, enterprising man, who was especially successful in rearing fine lambs; thereby giving his old bachelor brother the tanner, plenty of employment in dressing the hides and fleeces, thus keeping "two mills going at once," as he said. The old tanner had a trade secret of his own for curing the skins in some peculiar way with the bark of the willows that grew so plentifully on the borders of the stream that ran through his tan yards. No one's hides sold so readily as old Johann Nilson's, or fetched so good a price in the market. They were entirely reserved for making gloves, and exported to England for that purpose. CENTRAL

The next two sections of my figure are, as you see, of a bright scarlet colour; and, like those two on the opposite side, which are of a rich dark blue, are made of morocco leather. This is made from the skin of Spanish goats, carefully tanned with oak bark, and then dyed on the grain side. The crimson portion owes its hue to being steeped in a bath with the little cochineal insect; and the blue to indigo. It is then curried and glazed till it becomes as shining and smooth as you see it.

Half of my fourth and last section is made of kid that was once pure white; and of the same kind as th   used for ladies' gloves and boots. But time a l rough usage have turned it now to a somewhat dingy hue. This was made from the skin of a calf, which was carefully steeped in baths of lime and bran, and then dressed with flour paste, and well stretched; being finally polished and smoothed with hot irons. This came from France, and after all this toil and care bestowed upon it, was beautifully soft and white, as supple as you could desire, and ready to be made into gloves. The other half of my last portion is formed of what is called chamois leather, being made from the skin of a lively little chamois that in vain once fled along Alpine peaks to escape his fleet hunter. The only part that now remains to account for is the small round portion at each end, which, from its dark, peculiar, tawny hue and pleasant scent, you have no doubt recognised as Russia leather. This, which is so highly prized because insects will not destroy it, or damp penetrate through it, owes much of its virtue to its being tanned with the bark of the graceful birch tree.

I have now, I think, satisfied even my friend the Humming-top, and may proceed to tell you that these several portions of my frame, coming as they did from various countries, and owing their colour and texture to different ways of pre-paring them, were all stored together in a very large wholesale warehouse, in a narrow, gloomy lane in the heart of London. These were all sold out again to travel once more, some to the glove-making counties; others to great shoe factories; some to makers of dressing cases and purses; others to grocers in town or country for polishing plate and glass. With all this general separation, there were a good many stray pieces, some torn off by accident, others used for pattern samples, which were always carefully collected, down to the smallest bits, and put into an old box by the boy who swept the warehouse. His master allowed him to collect them each week and carry them home to his mother, a poor, industrious widow, who earned a scanty living for her children and herself by making toys for a shop in the suburbs.

The eldest son, Sam, was shop-boy at this great leather warehouse; and feeling the importance of his position as the man of the family, and the only one receiving regular wages, and being in a place, he was not a little proud. He drew himself up on tip-toe, for he was, unluckily, rather short for his age, and spoke in the deepest tones he could make his naturally squeaky voice take, which sounded like the chirp of the cuckoo, when "in leafy June, he is out of tune!" But Sam was a good boy, and loved his mother and little sisters dearly, and would have bristled, like an angry cock robin, in the smallest but fiercest displeasure, if any one had tried to invade the parent nest.

It was Saturday night, and Sam was very tired, for he was at everyone's call, being the

youngest and smallest there; and though he
was pert and perky, he was good-natured and
willing, so his poor thin legs had been well
trotted about. But tired as he was, he gave a
careful look round for any stray bits, and then
tucked his little old box under his arm, and
walked home. He stopped at the door of a very
dingy house, up a dark, dirty court, and opening
it, mounted the close, steep staircase. After
climbing up two stories, he sat down to rest
awhile, to get breath to mount the last one.
At last he wearily picked up the box, and, step
by step, painfully went up to the door of the
back room. And this was his *home*, his only
idea of comfort and rest after his long day's
toil. But his mother was a good and tender
woman, and though she had only this one small
room to dwell in, where her three children
and herself lived and slept, she tried her very
best to keep it as wholesome and cheerful as
she could, with the poor means she had.

A pleasant place it seemed to poor little Sam
as he went in, with the kettle singing merrily
on the hob, and the summer sunset shining in
over the tall chimney-pots, through a clean win-

dow, between two cracked pots of blooming
mignonette. Many little children were, no doubt,
going to bed then in country cottages, tired out
with their long rambles in country lanes—dirty
with dust and forbidden mud-pies—and hungry
for the crust of very dry bread—but healthy
from their day's long breathing of pure air.
But Sam only exchanged the close city warehouse, with its disagreeable smell of leather, for
that of a room in which his mother and sisters
breathed most of the day the smoky air among
the chimney tops. In he came, only too glad
to rest, and thankful for the warm tea his mother
had ready for him. And then he showed his
treasure of pieces of leather, such a big bundle
this time, that little Susan clapped her hands
quite gaily; and his mother said that there was
enough for a half score dozen of balls at least!

The poor widow made leather balls to sell to
a toy shop; her eldest girl, Jemima, always called
Jemmie, made little toy bedsteads, for she had
been lame from her birth. Little Susan, the
youngest, helped as well as she could by making
the little bolsters and mattresses for the dolls' bedsteads, which were to form the toys of luckier

and younger children. She was a grave little morsel, with long thin, *thin* limbs, and hollow cheeks—but she would have been pretty, with her large soft blue eyes and long yellow hair, if she had been well fed and healthy.

Their mother took the box of leather scraps from Sam, and having made him comfortable at his meagre tea, she began at once to arrange her work; for the last week she had quite used up all her scraps, and had been obliged to use her spare time in helping Jemmie with the bed-steads. So she picked out the colours, and laid her card patterns on them, and cut them with as little waste as possible, and as I was the first ball she finished that evening, I saw and heard all that ensued.

" Are you very tired Sam," she asked, "you're late home to-night. However, to-morrow is blessed Sunday, and you can take your rest with all the other poor creatures God has made His holiday for."

" Oh yes, mother," said Jemmie, her sallow face quite lighted up, " and we can have another walk in the Park, you know. Only I wish I could walk better, it is such slow work hopping along."

"So it is, Jemmie," replied her mother, sigh-
ing, "but thank God, child, you don't keep your
bed; that would break my heart. I hope it'll
please Him to spare me *that* sorrow, and then
I'll be contented if you can only crawl like a
snail."

"I wish it was treat time," said little Susan;
"oh, how we did enjoy it, mother! if only you
had been there! Oh, they were such grand trees
in the forest, mother, they seemed to reach up
to the clouds; I'm sure the birds could'nt build
their nests up there! Why they were three times
higher nor these chimbley stacks!"

"I liked the ride best," said Jemmie; "wasn't
it nice to be carried along like that, and resting
all the time; and teacher was so kind. She lent
me her thick shawl to sit on; and how nice it was.
What a lot of flowers we brought you, mother.
And how nice and dry our acorns have kept."

"When I'm only a little bit older," said Sam,
"and earn more money, we'll have such jaunts
into the country; won't it be fun to climb a tree,
and lie on the grass!"

The mother sighed wearily; but she en-
couraged the children to gossip on cheerfully,

for the work went twice as quick, while the memories were living over again the few, few days of fresh air and sunshine they had known. And the work *must* be done, for the sake of food and shelter, such as it was. As for clothes, they were not thought of; for they were darned, patched, and "tidied up," till they were *all* darn, and only replaced, when some kind friend gave a cast off garment. Jemmie made pretty little dolls' bedsteads, the frames of which, made of white wire, she bent into shape, and strengthened with slender strips of tin. Sam soldered them neatly together for her in his precious spare time, the wire and tin being sold to her cheap, cut ready into lengths, by a friendly tinman. Then Jemmie trimmed them up with white muslin worked round with gay coloured yarn. They were such pretty little toys that she found a tolerably ready sale for them.

"What a sight of work you've got for me, Jemmie!" said Sam, as his mother cleared away the tea, and his sister got out the wires. "A chap ought to have a lot of strength for such a nigger drivin missus as you!"

"Never mind, Sam," said Jemmie, cheerfully; "don't do no more nor you feels inclined

for. But Mr. Dobbs had such a lot of bits for
me this week, and as mother was slack of work,
she turned to and made up all the curtains and
valances, and I had only to do the wool work.
So we've got a sight of 'em done, and then, if
mother has time this week, she thought she'd
take a few round and sell 'em."

"So she shall!" said Sam, setting vigorously to work, "*I* don't mind, there's lots of
work yet in this here feller, all along of your
cup of tea, mother, and the holiday to-morrow."

"I think it wouldn't do no harm, Jemmie,"
said the widow, as she finished me, and laid me
aside, "if you was to send one of your bedsteads
to Mr. Nethersole's little Miss. He's kind to
Sam, and it seems only a dutiful way of thank-
ing for all these nice bits. You've got enough
and to spare."

"Take one and welcome, Sam," said Jemmie,
limping off to the cupboard and bringing one
out; "you shall have this here for little Miss.
It's the king of the lot, and is worked in the
last bit of magenter wool I've got."

Sam quite approved of this offering to his
ruling powers, and on Monday morning he set

off early to his work, refreshed and brightened by his brief holiday, and very proud of the bedstead, which he carried carefully in a paper bag.

It was duly presented, and not only admired, but brought Sam a message which made him tear home at headlong speed after his day's work, and face the stairs with the desperate energy that helps a soldier to storm a wall, and that carried Sam, hot and breathless, into the room to tell the good news in gasps that frightened Susan out of her wits, and nearly drove his mother frantic. At last, by patting his back, and making him sit in her low chair by the open window, the calmer Jemmie found out that Mrs. Nethersole had sent to say she liked the doll's bedstead so much that she should be glad to have three dozen like them, for which she would give five-and-twenty shillings a dozen, as she was going to have a stall at a very large bazaar, and had not much time to work for it herself.

" And you can make a lot of balls, mother, and she'll try and sell 'em for you, and will guarantee two dozen at sixpence each. She's a jolly brick, mother, that she is! But the best of it is to come, for they had me into the parlour and asked me all about us; and master has riz my wages a shilling a week. I'm the happiest chap in London, and I'll never call him "old skinny" no more, that I won't! Hurray, Jemmie! Up ye goes Sue."

"I am sorry, my friends," said the Ball, "I can tell you no more of them; for you see I was packed up with the rest and sent off to the Crystal Palace, where Mrs. Spenser bought me on the bazaar day, and I have lived among you ever since. But I should like to know how Sam, and Jemmie, and little Sue are getting on."

CHAPTER III.

THE HOOP'S ROUND OF ADVENTURES.

WHEN the Ball had concluded his story, and had modestly taken a leap backwards out of the way, he was eagerly accorded the warm thanks of the party, and desired in his turn to call upon some one else.

"I am sure I feel deeply honoured that you should be amused with my poor story, and hope sincerely that my successors will have something more interesting to relate. I will now call upon our merry friend the Hoop, to give us his experiences in life."

"O dear me," cried the Hoop, rolling slowly out of his corner, but contriving in his course to scatter the Marbles to all the corners of the room, and to knock down the Doll also. "My dear Doll, how sorry I am, alas! alas! I am so very unlucky in always doing awkward things."

"Oh," sighed the Doll, "I can't bear much more! I am almost gone now!"

"Come and sit on my roof," said the Noah's Ark, very compassionately, "it is not at all rickety, I can assure you, for *your* light weight; and I will keep you out of all harm." And so he carefully consoled and took care of the poor old Doll.

"I don't think awkwardness goes by luck," snapped the Shuttlecock; "people need not be clumsy unless they choose. It is carelessness, and giddiness, that cause all these mishaps!"

"I daresay you are right," said the Hoop, candidly, "I always was a giddy young thing. But where are all the Marbles gone! poor little fellows; I must go and help them back!"

"You had much better stay where you are!" whispered the Ball, "you'll only get into fresh scrapes; there's the Kite just in your way, and if you poke a hole in his head, you won't hear the last of it in a hurry, I'll promise you!"

So the Hoop edged himself into a corner, where he stood safely propped against the door, for although he was a careless, awkward fellow, he was really very goodnatured, and would not vex any one on purpose.

"I have really no story to tell you," said he; "for, as you see, I am simply a large iron ring, and could not have been very difficult to make. And as to any relation of my round of adventures, they are, I am sorry to say, only one long list of accidents and mishaps. But as our good friend the Ball has set us all a noble example by so readily obliging the company, I will also do my best. My first step in life was to be hung with several of my companions at the door of a toy shop at Sydenham. Here, however, I did not stay long, for I was selected by a little boy, called Edward Moore, who had saved up his pocket money for many weeks in order to purchase me. My first unfortunate beginning occurred almost at the shop door, for Master Teddy, in all the rapture of first calling me "his very own," gave me such an energetic tap with the new stick, that I went over the smooth pavement as if I had been oiled; ran sharply over an old gentleman's gouty foot, and only checked myself in my mad career by slipping through some railings, and tumbling down a strange area.

I could see nothing at first, but heard the old gentleman bawling angrily for the police; but, very luckily, as usual, none happened to be about, and after a little while the hubbub subsided, and the old gentleman, after abusing and threatening my poor Teddy well, limped off, and my disconsolate owner had time to peep down the areas, and try to recover his lost property. I had no idea of remaining buried in that dismal den, so I managed to roll off the flower pot I had fallen on, and by the jangle attracted his attention. He rang the bell, and coaxed the maidservant to let him go down and fetch me.

"Get along with you, yer impedent monkey, a-ringing at people's bells, and a-calling one up in the middle of cooking! I shan't let you in! *I* don't care for your hoop, nor you neither!"

"Oh, do Mary! there's a kind girl," coaxed Teddy; "I know you're goodnatured, because you've got such a laughish mouth! *Do* give me my hoop, it's just new, and I've saved up for it ever so long, you can't think!"

"Bless the boy's imperence," said she, half laughing, "who told you my name was Mary, which it isn't, for it's Jane! You're very saucy, and have no call to make rude remarks about my mouth. Go along with with ye, there's your precious hoop!"

And so saying, she gave me a toss which sent me spinning up into daylight again, and nearly knocked off a grand young lady's smart hat, who walked grumbling off, looking daggers at Teddy, and muttering something about "pests of children!"

Teddy, however, was too rejoiced to regain me to care for anything else, and shouting his thanks to Jane, he set off home at a good pace, taking me on his arm till he got out of the paved street into the green lanes. And here for many a day we ran races, and one of us at least was mightily tired. At last, one unlucky day Teddy's mother sent him on an errand to a shop in the middle of the most frequented street, and he had now become so used to his indispensable companion, that he took me with him, of course. We went, on very merrily, till we came to the corner of a crossing, when, thinking he could send me over before a great coal waggon came too near, Teddy gave me such a tap that I bounded over the street in no time. But the curb stone tripped me up first, and in hopping over that I took an unfortunate slide, and rolled into the open door of a china shop. Before I could stop myself I had knocked down two jugs, run over a pile of plates, and fallen into the middle of an array of wineglasses, just newly unpacked from a great crate close by.

I am used to misfortunes now, and am of a very buoyant disposition, but never shall I forget the crash and smash of that early calamity. Teddy stood aghast for one brief instant, and then turned to run away, even forgetting *me* in the catastrophe. But that short moment had been enough to satisfy the horrified china merchant as to the author of the damage, and making a rapid spring across the road, he seized Teddy by the collar, and sternly hauled him into the shop. The poor boy was bewildered by the sudden accident, and half deafened by the shrill scolding of Mrs. Delf, who, having heard the crash, had rushed into the fray, and was now picking up the pieces.

"Two of the best Parian jugs!—I thought the police seized all the hoops as was seen,—nine willow cheeseplates,—and oh my! what a sight of glasses! You've done it now, and no mistake, you little vagabond!"

Her husband, however, seeing that Teddy was evidently a gentleman's son, after a few threats of fetching the police, decided upon accompanying him home, with a bill of the damages. Teddy begged and implored to be let off with many tears, but the man was determined, and taking me in one hand, he laid the other on Teddy's shoulder, and marched off in the direction of Willow Lodge, with the bill in his pocket. I must really draw a veil over the dreadful picture of the scene there, as my feelings will not allow me to do justice to the anger of Teddy's father, and the horror of his mother, at the money they had to pay for *that* accident. Let it suffice that poor Teddy had a whipping that cured his roving propensities for some time, and I was confiscated, and placed in ignominious imprisonment in the stable.

Some months must have elapsed in the meanwhile, for when I was first shut up it was the end of the late summer, and when I saw daylight again it was spring-time, for the lilacs and laburnums were in full flower. How glad

I was to rub off a little of the rust I had acquired
from lying so long in that damp place, and how
delighted was Teddy once more to get hold of
me.

"I tell you what it is, old fellow," said Teddy,
rubbing me industriously with his pocket handkerchief; "you must not let me into any more
scrapes, for I could only get you again by promising Ma to be very careful, and only take
you in the lanes. So we must mind what we
are about!"

And so we did; and were as sober and steady
as possible; perhaps, now that I was a little rusty
from want of exercise, I was not as nimble as I
used to be, but we got on very well, very comfortably indeed, and I began to think our
troubles were over, and that we were getting
older and more sedate. We had a few minor
mishaps, but these were not of a serious order;
for instance, when I just happened to run against
little Polly Stubbs, a small toddling body of two
years old, and upset her. But, then, after all,
she was a very waddley sort of duck on her feet,
and was very good tempered, so after the first
shriek, she scrambled up with her little fat roley

poley body, and began to laugh. And Teddy was so delighted with her good temper, that he patted her dirty cheeks, and gave her such a big lump of gingerbread, out of his pocket (where it had been rubbed all crumbling with his marbles), that her cheeks stuck out on each side as if she had a swelled face, she had stuffed her mouth so full.

Then another day we found a charming shady lane with no house in sight, and not a sound of a carriage to be heard, and so off we went helter-skelter,—I gliding swiftly on in advance, like a slender snake, and Teddy tearing along behind with his short, stumpy legs, and his face as red as a full blown peony,—puffing like a pair of bellows. He had reached me after a long chase, and gave me a good bowl on, when we turned round a slight winding, and came right into the middle of a brood of young ducklings, with their fat majestic mother waddling after them. Oh there was a scatter, as I rushed into the middle of them like a steam-engine coming, express into a flock of sheep! Some tumbled headlong into the pond hard by, others scrambled off out of the way as they best could, while old mother duck quacked and waddled like one possessed. But one poor little lame duckling, the last of the troop, was just in my way. I could not stop myself, so the only thing I could do to prevent myself from killing or hurting her, was to fall, which I did, flat round her in the dusty road, to her infinite fright. But she was not hurt, and, after crouching down for a moment, she recovered, and scrambling weakly over my prostrate circle, she limped off to the pond, and then sailed off into deep water with a delighted quackle that amply repaid me.

Our next misfortune was worse; but it did not cause any serious consequences to us, although for a long time, warned by his previous experience, poor Teddy walked about with a grave face, and trembled at every ring of the bell. We were out as usual, and *had*, perhaps, put more steam on than was quite necessary, for it was one of those lovely fresh mornings in early June, that are as bracing as a glass of cold water, or a breath of pure air. Teddy was capering and dancing along, and had dealt me one of what he called his " left handers " which were awkward, uncertain strokes, that *I* privately christened "wobblers!" Well, he had just given me a wobbler, when a horrid pebble came in my way; and what business pebbles have in the way in the middle of a foot path *I* never could discover. They are quite out of their own track, and very much in the way of elderly ladies and gentlemen who have pet "callosities." Why, every toddling child tumbles over them, and as for *my* family, we abhor them! Let them be kept to their beaches, and brooks, and not interfere with our few surburban enjoyments! Well, as I was saying, when indignation got the better of me, I was turned *out* of my course by one of those hateful round, slippery pebbles, and *into* a strange garden, and a very smart one too! I slipped over the smooth, dewy grass like lightning, and right through a clump of hyacinths, ending my career by falling in a scrambling, all-four sort of fashion all over a bed of choice tulips. How many I beheaded I do not know, for Teddy, after peeping with a horrified face over the hedge, and seeing no one about, made a rush in to rescue me, and carrying me off, never stopped running till we were safe at home in the old stable.

As I said before, we were not found out in that instance, and, after a little seclusion, we came again into active life, when the crowning misery happened that parted me from my poor little master. We were going out quietly enough, and in a solitary lane too, turning as steadily as a rusty old windmill, so that I felt half asleep; when suddenly I was twirled about, whisked here and there, and then dropped in the dust, amidst such a confusion of shouting and screaming as beggars description. And this time it was owing to a donkey! This perverse animal, after having never been known from his youth to do more than walk. or jog-trot under any treatment whatever, had at this unlucky time taken it into his long-eared head to run away full gallop with his owner, a deaf old woman, hanging on to the front of the little cart, with all her market produce jumbled together as it had never been before. Down he came thundering upon us, and before poor Teddy could catch me up, while he had but scant time to get into the hedge himself, I got entangled in the wretched little brute's rough legs, and down we all came, old woman, donkey, cart, and all, with a perfect set of fire-works of onions, cabbages and potatoes, flying in the air all round us. The first thing I noticed after the general crash was Teddy, who sat in the hedge shrieking with laughter, and a funny appearance I daresay we all presented. The cart, with one wheel off, was dragged and knocked about by the wretched little donkey's struggles to regain his legs. But the old woman had been shot down on the top of him, and as she was very fat and heavy she lay there like a sack of beans, only uttering fearful moans and shouts, with her face covered with bruised strawberries, and a shower of green peas all over her.

Teddy scrambled out of the hedge and very kindly helped up the old woman and her donkey, and collected all her stray vegetables as well as he could, for he was a very good-hearted boy, in spite of his carelessness. But the crabbed old woman laid all the blame on him, and follow-ing him slily home, beset the house, and made such a fuss, that Teddy got in the wars again worse than ever. His mother believed his ac-count of the mischief, because, with all his faults, he was very truthful; but his father was very angry, and though he only paid the old woman half her outrageous demand, he punished Teddy severely, and wound up by depriving him of me altogether.

"Well Ma!" said poor Teddy, almost tearfully, "if I must not have my hoop myself, I know no one I'd sooner give it to than Frank Spenser, my old schoolfellow. Pa's so angry with me about it, I don't like to ask him; but if *you* would, I daresay he'd let Frank have it."

His mother, who was really sorry for him, did so very readily, and Teddy had the only satisfaction left him, in giving me to his friend. Frank was almost too old to care for a hoop, but he did not like to hurt the poor boy by refusing, so he took me with a very good grace, and promised to take great care of me; which he certainly has done by shutting me up here like this; and so now my friends I think I have related my whole round of adventures to you, as far as I can myself, remember.

CHAPTER IV.

THE FATE OF THE LEADEN TEA-THINGS.

THE rest of the Toys having thanked the Hoop for his story, he once more rolled himself lazily into a comfortable position, and took his rights by calling upon the leaden Teapot, to entertain them next. But such an uproar arose among all the leaden Tea-things; the cups and saucers, clattering and clanking like mad, and the milk jug even mounting on the sugar basin to be heard the better, that for a few moments no one could be heard. But the little Teapot set to work vigorously, and soon reduced her unruly family to order. She rolled one teacup here, and bowled over another there, piled up the plates before they knew where they were, and toppled down the milk jug into its proper place, before it recovered enough to defend itself. Then she sat down and volubly began her story, while her tribe were temporarily pacified.

"I am afraid," said she, "you will not like my story at all, for it's not half so lively and entertaining as the Hoop's, in fact there's nothing merry about it, but quite the reverse. I can tell you nothing of my birthplace or of my original history, for you see I've had a large family to keep together, and look after, and I've been so battered and knocked about in my course through life, that my memory is sadly impaired. So I can only tell you that we all came from Germany, where we were made, and were carefully packed in a little pasteboard box, in which we travelled to the English house to which we were sent, with numbers of others. We remained for some time in seclusion on the shelf of the toy warehouse, and were then drafted off to a little toy-shop at the West end of London. Our present owner was a notable little woman, the wife of a head workman at a large cabinet manufactory, and as she had two or three small children, she was glad to make ends meet by fitting out her front parlour as a little toy-shop. It was a very quiet, nice street, not far from a large hotel, and as the rents were rather high, the houses were only let to fairly respectable people. The little woman let her first floor, neatly, but plainly, furnished, to an elderly lady; and by all these small helps, added to her husband's wages, they lived very comfortably, and brought up their little ones nicely. A younger sister of the wife's lived with them, and was a great help in waiting on the old lady and in serving the customers.

Rose was such a good-tempered girl, she was a great favourite with all the young purchasers; she never cared what trouble she took to suit them, and turned over the whole stock of toys that she might find what they wanted. All the little poor children in the neighbourhood used to watch to see when she came into the shop to make their small bargains. She never grumbled while they picked out the prettiest faces that suited their fancy among the halfpenny wooden dolls, and she kept a choice corner of very cheap toys on purpose for all these little ones, who so rarely knew what the pleasure of buying a toy was. But I think she had her reward when she saw the little eyes nearly sparkle, and the pale,

thin faces get a little colour, as they trotted
happily off with their few and scanty treasures
cuddled up in their old ragged pinafores. We
lay for a long time on the counter with our lid
off, to tempt the young folks who came to the
shop, so I had some opportunity to see all the
different customers.

I suppose my own busy, careful life, with all
my tribe of young ones, has made me understand
all these things better, for I remember so much
of this time, while I have forgotten a great deal
else. How often I have seen the richer class of
children come in with their governesses or servants, and just glancing over the toys carelessly,
they have selected what they wanted, and have
gone off, with no more than a passing pleasure
with their possessions. And very likely in a
fortnight the same party have returned again,
and carried off something else, feeling more
careless than before at the sight of the playthings
they had almost exhausted.

Different to them, as station and dress could
make them, were Rose's little friends. The
golden hair, or dark braids of the little ladies,
and their flower-like faces, set off with their trim

hats, and tasteful, cool, well-made dresses, did not contrast more strongly with the sallow faces, ragged, short locks, tangled with wind and weather, and the patched or ragged garments of the poorer children, than did their manners and wants. These latter little ones were the small evening audience who flattened their noses against the bright, gas-lighted window of the gay toy-shop, and who knew all its contents by heart, as well as its owner. But they never hoped, poor little souls! except in dreams, for all these beautiful toys. Dirty little Polly, who stood pointing with her smutty finger, and elbowing her sister to look at the grand doll dressed in muslin and ribbon, only gazed at it in a sort of ecstatic rapture, and had no more idea, indeed far less, of having it for her very own, than little Lady Edith had of owning the Crystal Palace. Pence, scanty, hard-earned pence, were too much wanted for bread and food, to be easily got to lay out even in two half-penny dolls in a year! But when a happy piece of good fortune did come about, and these poor little creatures really had a whole penny they could call *their own*, oh, how difficult it was to spend it! How much they wanted for it! and what a business it was to decide what it should be laid out in! And the one-jointed doll or penny cart was like a pot of gold to its happy little owner for months afterwards!

Rose had other friends as well, however, as these poor little ragged customers, for her pleasant face and gentle voice made her popular with all, and she had a tasteful way of arranging the one window of the toy-shop that made it quite attractive to older eyes than the children. One day in late autumn, a lady, with a nurse and a little girl, paused before it for a moment, and after a brief inspection they came into the shop.

"I think a box of tea-things will be almost the best thing for her, Lee," said the lady to her nurse.

"I sould ike a bots of tea-sings wey mush!" said the little thing, as the servant sat down, and placed her on her lap.

"So you shall have some, my pet, and then you will be able to make tea for all the dollies," replied the nurse.

"Have you any boxes of wooden tea-things?" asked the lady.

Rose placed before them a tolerably large assortment; some made of china, very brightly ornamented with pink and blue flowers; some made of glass, white with tiny gold sprays and stars, but these were voted dangerous for baby, because they would break easily, and might cut her little fat hands. Then the wooden sets were examined, but they were painted freely, and mamma and nurse thought they might go to the rosy mouth more closely and often than would be quite wholesome, and baby would not look at the plain, white Swiss carved tea-sets, pretty as they were.

"Fower ike those, wey pitty," cried she, eagerly, as Rose brought out our box of large polished leaden tea-things.

"Then she shall have them!" decided Mamma at once, "and a very good choice too, Lee, don't you think so? They will be quite safe, and neither break nor spoil so easily as the rest. How much are they? I will take these please!"

And so Rose packed us carefully up in paper and gave us to the nurse, who, taking up the little girl, carefully tied on her warm fur cape and carried her after the lady. They walked for a short distance, and then stopped at the door of a house in a handsome square. The lady's beautiful dress and elegant air had somewhat prepared me for our new home, which was one of luxury. The lady, after tenderly kissing the little one, stopped at the door of her dressing room, while the nurse and my new owner mounted another flight, and reached the spacious and airy day nursery. The little rosy girl was rolled out of all her velvet wraps, and a very pretty snowy embroidered pinafore was put on her, after her glossy bright flaxen curls had been carefully arranged by the nurse. The little thing had borne all this very impatiently, and had fretted and fidgeted to get away to her new toys; but her nurse would not let her go till she was "made tidy," as she called it.

"You shall have your little table, Miss Lily," said she, "and make tea till bedtime afterwards, if you like, but you must stand still first, like a lady, and be made to look neat. Don't you know mamma never goes down to breakfast or dinner till Lance has dressed her and done her hair."

But when these operations were all over, Nurse set out the little table, and covered it with a clean towel for a table cloth, and placed Lily's pretty wicker chair beside it. And when the real nursery teatime came, she gave Lily a lump of sugar, broken into little bits with the scissors, and two nice, dry biscuits to play with. So fat little Lily was mightily contented, and spread out her toys, and played at making tea for her dolls, while she herself ate up the biscuits and sugar with great delight. And by-and-bye Mamma came up to see how all was going on, before she went down to dinner, and she found her pet, trotting round the little table and humming like a big humble bee.

And so the time went merrily by, and if we had a few misfortunes, still we got on pretty well. To be sure, I gained this great dint in my side owing to my little mistress setting the leg of her chair suddenly on me. And some of the saucers and plates were swept up with the dust, and thrown away by a new, careless nursery maid. But on the whole we were rather well off, for Nurse was a patient, orderly woman, and went round the day nursery every evening herself, picking up the pet's playthings and putting them away.

And as for dear little merry Lily, she grew and throve, like a sweet-tempered child as she was, as fair as her namesake blossoms. She had called herself "Fower" in her childish talk, because Lily was not easily managed by her little tongue, and she had quite understood that she was called after the pretty-looking, innocent, white flowers that blossomed in the same month as her birthday fell in, the merry month of May.

One unfortunate day when we had been there some time, to the amazement of Nurse, she got up in such a fretful, cross humour nothing would pacify her. This was unusual, and so was her turning away from her nice bread and milk, and crying peevishly when she was spoken to. The poor child was evidently ailing, and Nurse lost no time in sending down word of it to her mistress. The fond mother hurried upstairs, but little Lily would only cling to her and sob, and bury her flushed face on her shoulder. So the doctor was sent for in haste, and he came quickly, and pronounced that the little one was sickening for some illness; measles, *he hoped*, but he could not positively say. So poor Mamma sat there, and gave Lily the medicine, and tried to amuse her with setting us in order before her. But Lily pushed us all away so hastily that we rolled to all corners of the room, and Nurse was too busy and sad to pick us up in a hurry that day, or for many days after.

For poor little Lily grew worse, and the doctor pronounced it to be fever, and of a very severe kind. Days and days the little feverish head tossed wearily on the pillow, and then all the golden curls were cut off, matted as they were, and laid aside carefully in a drawer by poor Nurse, who cried over them as if her heart would break. The fever subsided, but the little exhausted body had not strength to recover from it, and she grew daily weaker, quite too weak to be removed to a fresh air. Poor Nurse picked us up one night, half unconsciously, and put us back in the old toy drawer, where we remained, till one afternoon she came hastily to fetch us out again. She carried us downstairs into the beautiful bed-room where Mrs. Arden slept. But both Papa and Mamma were too anxious about their only darling to be very particular about their own comfort, and so her father slept in his dressing-room close by, while the mother kept a ceaseless watch by the sick bed.

When the lid was taken off, and nurse turned us out on the white counterpane, I could hardly recognise my little mistress. Did these sunken cheeks and hollow eyes, these little wasted hands belong to the " Fower," as she had called herself? She was indeed a faded flower, a drooping lily, and her bright, golden curls were all gone, like her rosy, childish bloom. But sickness had not been able to subdue the innocent, loving nature and bright spirit; and though the smile on her pale little mouth made her mother turn away in tears, it was the same happy tone in the weak thread of a voice that whispered :—

" Fower make tea now! Fower been *so* sick, but see like some tea! mother make it now!" and the little head, shorn so sadly of its golden glories, fell back weakly on the pillow, and the sudden gleam of light died out of the blue eyes.

" Yes, dear one, mother *will* make tea for ' Flower,' so many cups; and when Lily gets better and grows a strong girl again, mother and she will have feasts every day, and all day long."

"Fower like that, but *so* tired;" breathed the little one, feebly, and so Nurse hastened to catch us all up from the bed, and hurriedly cramming us into the box, she put us on the dressing table.

Next day "Fower" seemed to brighten up a little, and when we were laid out on the bed, she took us up languidly, and pretended to drink. But she was soon weary, and even our slight weight was too heavy for the frail hand. And so day after day passed by with no great change, finding us each morning laid out on the bed, near the little weary hands, tired of doing nothing; and afternoon saw us gathered away, while the curtains were drawn across the window to keep out the bright glare of the spring sunshine. And day by day the tender mother hoped on, while the more experienced Nurse shook her head, and the skilful doctor was silent, though so *very* gentle with the anxious mother and the little drooping child.

At last a day came, one of the early ones in May, when even Lee thought Lily looked clearer and brighter. Papa brought in a bunch of the finest lilies of the valley from Covent Garden Market, and his poor, wan little "Fower" was delighted with them.

"It will be her birthday in a week," said her mother, cheerfully; "Papa must bring her some more then. I hope Lily will be better, and able to sit up then!"

"Fower have a gand tea party, and pum take, so fine! where's my tea-fings?"

Nurse brought out the pet playthings, and arranged them on the bed before little "Fower," and Papa went off in quite gay spirits to his business. And Mamma took out a little white frock she had been embroidering for "Fower's" birthday wear, and which had been laid away for a long while out of sight. Nurse seemed to have no very settled purpose in the work way, and stole quietly about, arranging everything in a still dreamy kind of fashion. Meanwhile little "Fower" lay back in the soft bed, supported on downy pillows, and with pale pink lined muslin curtains floating round her. Her blue eyes rested upon us with a bright, far-away look that did not last long, as the fingers of one hand played with us, the other holding the bunch of lilies.

Presently Nurse came rapidly over. "The dear child is fainting!" she said, as she held up the little shorn head.

"Fower thirsty!" murmured the little voice, like a faint sigh, as the blue eyes seemed to lose all their light, and the lilies dropped out of the open fingers.

"Lily, *my* Lily!" cried the poor mother, eagerly, "look up, my darling, you are better dear; let mother give her a little water out of her tiny teacup."

The kindhearted nurse laid down the heavy head, and spent all her heartfelt care now on her poor mistress. Her little "Fower" had gone in an angel's hand, to be planted a living blossom in her heavenly Father's garden, where her deep thirst would be satisfied quite, and the shining robe of the white lilies of heaven was waiting for her.

The little worn-out, earthly form was laid to rest with the bunch of lilies in the cold hands, and a wreath of fresh-gathered flowers on her head. And poor Nurse, thoughtfully gathered up all the toys that the little one had played with, and put them carefully out of the desolate mother's sight. And in after years I heard that other little blossoms came to fill up that grand nursery, but Nurse never loved them as she did little " Fower," and the mother gave her all the toys, very tearfully.

" I don't like to hoard them up," she said, " for after all I need no memorials to remind me of my Lily, and I like to think of her growing now a sweet, fair flower in her heavenly Father's garden, and yet I could not bear to see all these things played with and thrown about in the nursery. So take them, Nurse, and let them give pleasure to other little ones."

" And thus Nurse Lee took charge of us, and one evening coming to drink tea in Mrs. Spencer's nursery, she brought us all in our box for Miss Celia, who was then a little girl. But since she grew older, we were stuffed away by chance in this old cupboard. I told you all fairly that mine was a melancholy story," added the Teapot, in an injured sort of voice, " and you see I am right, and now I've done ! "

The rest of the Toys did not make much

remark, for they were all rather saddened by the story of little " Fower," but the Ball, who could not be very grave for long together, bounced up briskly, and told the Teapot, she was entitled to call on any of the rest of the company for a story in turn.

"I would rather not," replied the Teapot, eagerly; "I am but a foolish body at all such formal doings. Pray let the next in turn favour us."

Then the Ball, rather afraid of a discussion, turned it off with a joke and said:—

"Well, then, in your name I will call upon the Kite for a story, for, as he flies so high, he can't be very nervous, and no doubt he has seen a good deal in high latitudes, that we shall be glad to hear!"

The Kite waved a graceful bow all round, and professed his entire readiness to be at the service of the company.

CHAPTER V.

THE MAKING OF THE KITE BY THE HOME CIRCLE.

 " WILL begin," said he, " by describing my first appearance in my present form. Never did a large ship launch or the building of a great mansion require more care and pains, or entirely engross more workmen than I did in *my* construction. My architect-in-chief, I must tell you, was George Vernon, Esquire, commonly called 'Uncle Gee,' and the workmen he employed under his orders were as follows. Foreman, or rather forewoman, Mrs. Tufnell, otherwise called indifferently, mother, mamma, or mummy; and as workpeople, Bob, aged eleven; Tom, aged ten; Mary, alias Polly, aged nine; Jeanie, usually termed 'Jean' aged eight; Theodore, popularly christened 'Dora,' because he was a little given to tearfulness and whines, aged seven; and lastly little

Lucy, who still bore the name of " baby," and who numbered five summers.

Now Uncle Gee had come home for his holidays, for though he was nearly grown up, and seemed a giant in cleverness to all his little nephews and nieces, he was still at Oxford, and working hard at his studies. But he was very fond of all the little folks at Summerfield Rectory, and the days to the long vacation were nearly as eagerly counted by Uncle Gee, even amidst his more serious business, as by the flock of eager little adorers at the quiet home in the west. Everything that was nice and pleasant was deferred until his arrival, and a queer variety of treasures were hoarded up for his inspection long before he came.

And Uncle Gee amply rewarded his faithful adherents, for when he came, he brought universal sunshine with him, and was as ready to enter into all their pursuits and share all their games as the veriest child amongst them. He was the best teacher of trapbat and rounders Bob and Tom knew for miles round; and yet he was as skilful and neathanded at repairing the damages in Mary's doll house, and the fractures

F

of baby's doll, so that he might have been a carpenter by trade.

So when at teatime, one summer evening, Mamma said to the children, who were all round the large long table, "To-morrow Uncle Gee is coming!" they all burst out in one regular shout of delight, for this time he had gone on a visit to a friend first, and his young relations' calculations had been all put out, and they had been waiting day after day in the vain hope of seeing him. The noise and chatter round the tea table that evening were really deafening, and would have been quite annoying to anyone but Mamma, who smiled, and said it was a little taste of preparation for the uproar that always lasted all through Uncle Gee's visit.

And next day he came, to the great delight of all the young folks, and if he had been nearly as patient as Mamma, and quite as brave as Papa, (who did not even fear mad bulls, said baby!) why he would have been driven deaf, dumb, and blind, by all the voices talking in their loudest keys at once, or else would have expected to be torn in pieces by all the eager hands that clung to him and pulled him about.

I think Papa and Mamma, and Uncle Gee too, in spite of all their kindness and affection for the uproarious little mob, were thankful enough when the children's bedtime came, and they were all taken off, loudly declaring that it was *not* time yet.

Next morning they were all up like larks, and had finished dressing sooner than usual, but, to their great horror, they looked out and saw the sky covered with leaden clouds, and heard the steady, heavy drops of rain falling on the skylight over the staircase.

"What a nuisance," growled Bob and Tom, "when we wanted to try the new field, and Uncle Gee promised to have a game of cricket with us!"

"O dear," said Mary, in dismay, "and I wanted to show him the new hammock swing Papa has given us!"

"We've lost our swing for certain," said Jeanie, who was a regular romp; "what a bother!"

"Rain, rain, go to Spain," chanted Baby, in her squeaky voice—while Dora joined in chorus.

"Who's singing that contraband rhyme?"

said Papa, coming in ; " I'm too thankful for the rain for the sake of my peas and potatoes !"

" And the strawberries too," chimed in Mamma; "just think, children, how they were shrivelling for want of rain.

" But we can't get out," bawled all the children, " and now Uncle Gee's come we had such lots of things to show him !

" What's the matter now ?" said Uncle Gee, coming in. " All this racket about a little rain ! Why, I was just thinking, while I was dressing, what a jolly day it would be to make a Kite !"

" Make a Kite !" shouted Bob; "O how stunning; O Uncle Gee, can you show us how to do it ?"

" I think I can, Bob," replied his Uncle, " but at any rate we'll try, and with Mamma's help perhaps we can manage it. I dare say she will let us have the school-room to make all our litters in, and I shall want every man jack of you to help !"

" Am I man jack too, Uncle Gee ?" asked Baby, very anxiously.

" I should think so," said Uncle Gee, kissing her, " a very useful one too; you shall help with the fine fringy tail !"

And when breakfast was over, to work they all went. Papa found some capital slips of light thin wood, and lent his best knife into the bargain. Mamma contributed some beautiful white glazed lining to cover the frame with, and lent her nice glue pot as well. Uncle Gee soon had the long table in the school-room covered with all sorts of things, and had set everybody to work as well. Bob and Tom busily hammered, fixed, planed, and cut, till they hindered Uncle Gee terribly; and when he saw Mary take up the scissors, and begin to measure the calico, he stopped short, and called a truce.

"Now," said he, "if all are going to be at work, and no one master, we shall soon get into a fix, and knock over the whole concern. If we are to get the Kite made to-day, you must all obey orders. Mary, you and Jeanie can find me some strips of coloured paper, can't you, for the tail; and Dora, ask Nelson if she can let us have a long ball of string."

And so the work went on merrily. Bob and Tom doing the looking on, and Mary and Jean smoothing and snipping the bits for the tail, and making the tassel for the end. Dora fetched out a box of colours of his own, and suggested painting a face on it.

"Capital!" cried Uncle Gee; "and I'll tell you how you can make yourself useful, Dora, and that's by rubbing up a lot of colour on the back of a clean plate, I'll show you how;" and so to work Dora went with a will, and soon had a rare quantity all ready for the skilful hand of the artist.

Meanwhile, under Uncle Gee's superintendence, and with Mamma's help, Polly and Jean had supplied the long piece of string, provided for the tail with its cross pieces of paper to serve as light weights, and they were now busily snipping some very fine red paper Mamma had routed out from amongst her hoards for them, in order to make a grand tassel to finish the tail with.

"Does not this remind you of our own old days?" said Mamma to Uncle Gee, as she came in for awhile to help in the interval of her busy morning occupations.

"Don't you remember what trouble we used to take with our toys and playthings; and how seldom we were able to buy any real toys. I *do* think children have many more than are good for them," continued she.

"Well, they don't value them now, as we did our patched up contrivances, do they?" replied George; "but look, sister, won't this be a capital Kite? I think I never made a better, e'en in my boyish days! I am sure it ought to fly well!"

And so saying, he raised up the large, care·fully planned framework of slips of wood, with the calico neatly glued on it.

"I am going to leave it to dry now," said Uncle Gee; "I can't paint it while it is wet; and so now, young people, as I have worked in your service all the morning, it is high time you did for mine. I am going to write a letter, and have no more time to spare until after lunch. So you must promise me to leave this table un-touched, and go and amuse yourselves until by-and-bye."

The children agreed to this very fair bargain, and very sensibly dispersed, and amused them-selves until lunch time, which was really their dinner time.

When they all came down with carefully

brushed hair, and shining, clean faces, and took
their places round the great table, they were
about as merry a party as you would find anywhere, in spite of the drenching rain, which had
poured steadily on the whole day.

"The Kite is getting beautifully dry and
tight," said Uncle George, as he took the place
left for him; "I peeped into the school-room as
I came down, and I see it is drying fast and
nicely. And what shall we make it? A flying
dragon, like the Chinese flags and lanterns?"

"O yes! Uncle Gee," cried Dora, with his
eyes as round as cricket balls; "do make it a
dragon—a green dragon, with a fiery tail!"

"Or a likeness—warranted genuine—of old
Bogey himself," laughed Bob.

"A fairy with wings," suggested Mary," with
a star on her forehead, and a girdle round her
waist."

"Or a ship," said Jeanie, her dark face glowing; "a ship with masts and sails painted for
her, because you know she *does* sail through
the air, Uncle Gee!"

"Paint it like a daisy," said Baby, " or make
buttercups all over it!"

"Well, we'll see," said Uncle Gee; "when dinner is over we'll have a solemn council on the matter, and the most votes shall carry the day."

"Can anyone tell me anything particular about a Kite?" enquired Papa; "I think there ought to be a story somewhere; does anyone know it?"

"I do," cried Tom, eagerly; "Dr. Franklin found out about lightning with a Kite, didn't he?"

"Yes," replied Papa, "you are right Tom; but what did he find out by it, and how? Do you know?"

"No," said Tom, frankly; "I only remember he made a Kite to find out something he wanted to know about lightning, and there was something about a key, but I don't remember, Papa."

"I am glad you recollected a little about it," said Papa, "and I will tell you what the story was. Franklin, as you know, had long studied the effect of storms, and what is called Electricity. He was busied with setting some plans to work, which would enable him to try some experiments on the subject. But one day, while he was thinking over the matter, it flashed across

his mind that a kite, such as he had seen his
boys playing with, might help him to solve the
puzzle.   So he made one, not like yours, but
out of a silk handkerchief, and fixed an iron
point to the end of his stick, and where his string
ended he hung a key.   During the next thunderstorm that happened he went out and flew his
kite ; and by these simple means found out what
he had wanted to know.   You would hardly understand what the question was, or how it was
explained to him in this way, until you are rather
older, and are able to understand a little more
of all the curious phenomena of electricity.   You
are all very much frightened and roused when
we have a heavy thunderstorm, because it is such
a terrible thing, that you see the danger, but
some day you will know that the electric tele-
graph we send messages by is the same power
in a smaller, far smaller degree, turned to man's
use.   It is only God who can send the severe
thunderstorm, which while it clears and purifies
the air, and thus does a great deal of good, may
also do a great deal of harm; and to save some
of this was, shortly, the object of Franklin's
enquiries.   He saw that if his idea was correct,

rods of iron might be planted near houses, or suspended from vessels, by which means the lightning would pass harmlessly down into the water or the earth."

"And now," said Uncle Gee, "we must thank Papa for his lesson, children, and a very good one it is, and go to our work. I think if you were all to ask Papa very nicely, he might perhaps give you a simple explanation about thunder and lightning; and I daresay his school children would not be sorry to hear it too."

Papa promised to "think about it," and then off went the happy party into the school-room, where they found the great Kite stretched out like a large white bird or a windmill sail. Very dry, and nice and flat it was, and delighted enough they all were with it.

"Now," said Uncle Gee, " once for all what is it to be? A ship, a dragon, a Chinaman, or what? It is to be put to the vote—what do you say, Bob, you are the eldest?"

"What you like, Uncle Gee! A dragon would be a jolly thing, but let it be as you like!"

"I should like a ship," said Tom; "a big ship, with sails and an anchor!"

"We would rather leave it to Uncle Gee," said the girls and Dora; "he is sure to make a capital thing of it, and he has an idea of something or other, we think!"

"I shall make it into a flying fish, if you leave it to me," said Uncle Gee, laughing, "so you had better arrange it among yourselves."

And so there was a great deal of talking and chattering among them all, and at last they agreed to ask Uncle Gee to make it a bird.

"We can't settle what kind of bird it is to be," said Bob; "I wanted an eagle, but Tom liked an owl better, and Mary said she liked a ringdove, while Jeanie said it must be a peacock. Dora wanted a swan, and Baby bawled out for a robin! So we're not agreed in anything but that it is to be a bird. So you must decide out of all the number, Uncle Gee."

"All right," was Uncle Gee's reply, and to work he went and painted away vigorously to the young ones' great delight, while they all looked on and made remarks as he sketched in the outline. But they begun to press round him so, and make such queer suggestions, that he declared he would not do another stroke till they left him alone. So off they went to the other end of the table, and got the tail in order. It was a tail indeed! made of stripes of all coloured paper tied up, and ending with a tassel of various colours, whose fringes were feathery and full enough for a mandarin's pigtail.

By the time that the tail was finished to the satisfaction of all, Uncle Gee had completed the Kite, and turning it round to the children, exhibited a bird of such a kind as had never been seen before! It had the head of an owl, with its great staring eyes, the broad wings of an eagle, the neck of the ringdove, the ruddy breast of the robin, the many-eyed tail of the peacock, and the yellow webbed feet of the swan!

The children gazed at it for a moment in utter surprise, and then burst into shouts of approval.

"There," said Uncle Gee, "I hope I have satisfied you all, and every one in particular. I am sure such a bird as this would make his fortune at the Zoological Gardens!"

"Oh! what a jolly fellow!" shouted Bob and Tom, clapping their hands, while the girls danced round quite delighted.

"Now," said Uncle Gee, "I think to-morrow

will be a fine day after the rain, and we shall be able to make this fine fellow fly."

So they tied on my tail, and made me thoroughly ready for the next morning's cruise, and then all went to bed the happiest set of little ones within fifty miles round.

Many a flight I had with them over field and fallow, meadow and moor; many a dance I led them, and many a tree have I got entangled with, so that at last Bob became quite expert at climbing trees, and all owing to the practice he had in getting me out of scrapes. But time passed on, and when Bob and Tom went to school, Uncle Gee thought it was not safe to trust me to Dora and the girls, so he promised to make them another some day, and he gave me to the Spensers! So here you have an end of my history, which contains, as you see now, no flying adventures at all. If I had time, I could tell you of many curious things I saw in my airy flights, and some about the clouds I went so near. But I must defer that until another day, and meanwhile, in my turn, I ask our charming friend the Doll to oblige us with the account of her experiences in life.

CHAPTER VI.

THE DOLL AND ALL HER MISTRESSES.

"OH," said the Doll, "can you not excuse me? My poor little story is so very dull and flat after all we have heard, and, indeed, I am afraid I have not strength or vivacity enough to carry it through to the end!"

"No, indeed," replied the Ball, "we are not going to let you off. We are all of us taking our turns, and you must bear your share like the rest."

"I am sure," said the Kite, in a pacifying manner, "our fair friend will be only too happy to do her part in this pleasant task; she merely feels an amiable modesty, and undervalues her own charming powers."

"You flatter me too much," replied the Doll, "in all respects but one. But you are right in believing I am anxious to oblige every one, for that is the case really. And so now I will do my best, only prefacing my humble story by saying that I really know nothing of my origin, or where I was made. My first conscious remembrance was that of lying on a beautiful carved table in the midst of a quantity of silk and lace. Two or three gay girls were sitting round the table and gossiping merrily, while their busy fingers flew at their pretty work. They were dressing myself and one or two of my sisters for their Christmas tree."

"That is a piece of the first silk dress I ever had," said bright-haired Madeline, the eldest of them; "I remember how proud I was of it, and how I enjoyed its rustle. It was short, you know, Laura, for I was a little girl then."

"You don't care so much about silk dresses now, Maddy," replied Laura; "I think a new riding habit is your present ambition, isn't it?"

"This piece will make the doll a very grand bodice," said Edith; "the pale blue suits her complexion, don't you think so, Maddy? That is a piece of my last year's sash."

And so they chatted and worked, till I was

attired in a very tasteful and fashionable manner. For though, alas! there are now no remains of my former charms, I was reckoned a great beauty in my day, and was indeed quite one of the belles of the season. I had real hair, very soft and flaxen, and what is more, real eyelashes and eyebrows! You can see no trace of them now, for reasons I will relate presently. But without vanity, I may say I was charmingly pretty in those days, for I was the real model of a sweet fat baby child of about two years old. My face, neck, arms and feet had all the pretty wrinkles and dimples that adorn that age; and the soft pink wax, delicately coloured, gave a very fair notion of the tender pinky skin. So with very good taste my lady milliners dressed me in a short full white India muslin frock over a pale blue silk slip, trimmed the bodice and sleeves lavishly with sashes, bows, and loops of the same, and tied a pretty blue ribbon carelessly through my very natural curls. My attire was completed by white open work socks, and blue kid shoes; but Maddy crowned all her work by her last addition. Running hastily upstairs, she brought down a little box of small pearl beads, and after being seated at a remote table by herself for half an hour, while her friends were busily employed in giving the finishing touches to another of our company. who was attired as Red Riding Hood, she came suddenly forward, saying gaily,—

"I think I have added a last grace to *my* doll that ought to be irresistible, and make her the admired of all beholders."

And she showed on the tip of her finger a dainty little straw hat, coquettishly trimmed with a band of blue velvet, with a drooping fringe of blonde round the rim, having pearl drops to each point of the lace.

I was duly admired, and on the eventful evening was considered the prettiest doll on the tree, and many a little childish face cast longing eyes upon me, vainly hoping I might fall to her lot. But mine was a different destiny—a far higher one, as I imagined then! A dainty, lace-bordered ticket on my skirt showed that I was intended for Lady Alicia Wentworth, the little god-daughter of the lady of the house. After the festive evening was over, with all its glare of bright lights, and sounds of young voices and gay music, I was taken down from my proud position, which had not been free from peril, owing to the dangerous neighbourhood of the lighted tapers to my flimsy skirts. Little Lady Alicia lived too far off, and was too fully engrossed with the gaieties of her own immediate surroundings, to come to the party; and therefore I was most carefully packed in silver paper and wool, and sent to her.

My first little mistress was not by any means a very engaging child. She was very sickly, which perhaps rendered her more fretful than she would otherwise have been; but she would not have been so peevish, except for the fact that, as an only child, she had been spoiled and indulged to such an extent, that she could neither be happy nor contented herself, nor allow any one near her to be so either. When the lid of the box was opened, she, with a little momentary eagerness for the new toy, pulled off the silver paper and wool, and brought me out of my travelling box.

"It's a horrid Baby Doll," she exclaimed, in a loud tone of angry disappointment, "a stupid, old-fashioned, ugly Baby Doll! and I hate them, horrid, stupid things; what did they send me that for?" and she burst into a roar of passionate ill-temper. In vain did governess and maid try to pacify her; she screamed and pouted till her foolish, doting mother was obliged to sacrifice some visits she was going to make in order to drive in with her spoiled child to the nearest toy-shop, to purchase an expensive and more gaily-attired doll.

"I can't think what Mrs. Levesque could have been thinking of," she murmured, pettishly, as she got into the carriage again, "to send Alicia such a foolish thing, after making such a fuss about it too! It has vexed the poor little thing so, and upset her too much, which Dr. Blueby says is *so* bad for her!"

So when they returned home, Alicia went off with her new purchase, for a few hours of good humour and peace, while her ladyship desired the governess to pack me up in the box, and send me down with her compliments to the Rectory, to Dr. Stewart's little daughter, Flora. I found my new home much more to my taste; for, although also an only child, this little maiden was of a very different mind to the other. She was more delicate in health than the young lady at the Castle, for from a serious weakness of the spine she was obliged to lie down for many hours in the day, and was not able to run about and enjoy herself in the garden, as she often wished to do. But she was a naturally even-tempered child, and although she had long been motherless, her wise father had been a tender and judicious guardian, and her old nurse, who had watched over her from babyhood, lovedher as a child of her own.

I was amply repaid for the slights and affronts I had experienced from Lady Alicia, when I was carried in my box to the reclining board where Flora was then lying, for her father, delighted enough to bring his patient little girl a new pleasure, carried me in himself, saying,—

"Flora, here is a New Year's gift for you from the Castle. It is very kind of Lady Ennismore to remember my little girl. I am almost inclined to think it is a doll, my dear," he added, as Flora sat up and took the box, her thin hands trembling with eager joy, and her sallow face flushing at the sight. When I was revealed to her, she gave one rapturous exclamation, and hugged me affectionately to her.

"O Papa, a doll, a real Baby Doll, and dressed in such lovely clothes! Did you ever see anything so beautiful! Oh, how kind of Lady Ennismore. I suppose she had some down for Lady Alicia to choose from."

"It was very thoughtful and kind of her to remember you, Flora, and I must go and thank her for the great pleasure she has given you."

Then nurse was summoned, and expected to go over all the beauties of the new doll half a dozen times at least; my hair, my eyelashes, and my dimpled neck and arms received their full share of admiration. Nothing could have more enraptured Flora, for she was the greatest baby worshipper in the parish, and many a poor little nursling owed most of its occasional treats to the petitions of Flora. And so now my happy life began. I was carefully nestled up every night on a soft pillow, covered with a fine pocket-handkerchief, and only handled and nursed in the most careful way in the world. I lived with little Flora Stewart for six years, and was in nearly as good condition at the end of the time as at first. It is true, my complexion was somewhat tarnished by the air and dust, and my hair had become a little thinner, but no careless scratch defaced my countenance, or awkward fracture had injured my frail limbs. My fine muslin frock, indeed, had been frequently washed, and my hat cleaned and re-trimmed, while a pretty silk mantle added to my wardrobe, hid a good deal of the faded hue of my azure decorations. But for the last two years I had been laid away carefully in a drawer, for Flora had long ceased playing with me, and valued me more as a treasure of her childish days than anything else. She was now a tall, slender girl of nearly eighteen, having by the aid of all the watchful care spent on her earlier years quite outgrown the tendency to disease that had so threatened her childhood. She had grown up with the same sweet, unselfish nature though, and old affection for little children that had been so remarkable even in her early years; only that now she was able to be out among them all, and she might frequently be seen, the centre of a group of eager school children, all striving for her notice, while the babes in the cottages, who could not speak yet, would greet her with a crow and a spring as they were taken in her gentle arms. I have never seen my dear second mistress since our parting; but I have heard that she has little ones of her own now to love and care for, although they do not engross all her thoughts, for the little dark-skinned Hindoos will run to meet her as eagerly as her old school-class used to do; for she married a clergyman, who went out to India, and she has never returned home since. Dr. Stewart died long before her departure, and the old Rectory home was broken up; and when that happened, Flora gave me to a little child friend of hers, called Christie Johnson.

My third mistress was the greatest trial I had; for though she loved me dearly in a hasty sort of way, she was such a Tomboy, and so thoughtless, that under her charge I fell into numberless sad scrapes and accidents. Once I was dropped in the bath by Harold, her little brother, thereby losing what colour remained to me; and another time I was run over by a waggon, having been dropped out of the baby's perambulator, where I had been hastily placed, while Christie ran off to look for a bird's nest in a thorn bush. Under the awful crushing progress of that broad wheeled waggon both my wax arms and one of my legs were hopelessly smashed flat in the dusty road, my head and chest escaping by a miracle. Christie was terribly vexed at the catastrophe, but that did not mend my legs and arms, and I have therefore ever since led a miserable maimed existence. And the worst of it was that Alan and Willie had lost all respect for me, and never thought it necessary to be even commonly civil to me, now that my wax arms and legs were gone. I say *legs* purposely, for my sole remaining limb came to pieces by a fall down stairs. From that time my degradation commenced, and my daily existence was a miserable series of petty tortures, such as the ingenuity of a boy could alone devise. I was now the helpless and defenceless prey of those foes of our race; for Christie, although she occasionally rescued me from utter destruction, was too much of a romp herself, and too careless to look after my welfare thoroughly !

And so I found myself now continually reduced to becoming a frequent and convenient missile to the boys during their incessant wars and struggles. The stumps of my legs and arms were so very convenient to lay hold of, as they swung me round their heads, before sending me whirling through the air, or as they more forcibly than eloquently expressed it,—

" Christie's torso of a doll is such a jolly thing to chuck at a fellow, when you can't hit him ! "

Even little Harold, the two-year-old baby, who could not achieve such feats as these, could drag me about, as he did, by my poor stumps of legs, and cry, " Who buy ducks? I dot ducks a sell ! "

The life I led in that riotous nursery was indeed an ordeal, and during its course not only my few remaining charms were obliterated, like my eyes, which were perseveringly rattled into the back of my head by Ethel, but my wardrobe also vanished piecemeal. First my shoes went one by one, and the socks followed, no one knew how or where, but they were most probably dropped out of doors somewhere, like my hat, which took flight in a rough wind at the seaside! For Christie's mode of carrying me when she took me out for a walk was original certainly, but not a model to be recommended to mothers of live dolls. She would tuck me roughly under one arm, without taking any trouble to see whether my head or my feet were uppermost, and would then set off at the round trot for which she was famous, and that had earned from her brothers her nickname, "the postman."

The fictitious illnesses I have gone through would have furnished patients for the largest hospital in the world, but my last indisposition was of a character that made a more permanent alteration even in me. Now measles of a very malignant kind were at that time raging in the neighbourhood, and Christie's mother was very particular in keeping her children as much as possible out of the infection. Ethel, Christie's youngest sister, a child of about six years of age, had heard this talked over in parlour and nursery, and had imbibed a secret terror of this mysterious sickness which seemed so much

dreaded by mother and nurse. And if mothers
and nurses only suspected how *very* long the ears
of little pitchers really are, and how much more
they are inclined to take in all that *should* not
concern them, I think they would be as careful
as the House of Commons in sending out all in-
truders when serious questions were debated in
committee. I am only a doll, and have therefore no vote in the matter, or else if I *had* a
voice in the counsels of Home Government, I
would suggest that the little ears which take in
lessons and let them out again on the other side,
and which have yet the power of catching and
retaining all matters *not* necessary to their in--
struction, should be excluded from all graver
deliberations.

But this is a digression, and as it is one that
belongs to a world beyond our little kingdom,
it is perhaps not quite my business to enter on
it at all. Where was I in my story? I am
quite ashamed of trespassing so on your
patience; but time and hard usage have
so enfeebled my poor broken memory, that I
almost forget all I am doing or saying!"

"You were mentioning a serious illness that

occurred to you," suggested the Humming Top, very gravely; "pray relieve our minds as to its symptoms and duration!"

"Oh yes," resumed the Doll, languidly; "I was telling you how I really had the measles when they were so prevalent in our neighbourhood. Ethel, as I said before, was terribly alarmed at the vague disease; and not at all pleased with Baby Harold, who trotted soberly about the nursery, singing in his fashion,

"I dowing a have a measoos a morrer!" till Ethel got hold of him, and drew such an awful picture of what she imagined they must be, including a plentiful allowance of powders, currant jam, and castor oil, that he roared in terror.

"What's the row here?" asked Alan, lounging in at the time, and throwing himself full length on the hearth rug.

"I dowing a have a measoos, and Efel says I sall be sick—so bad—and Smif dive me powders!" sobbed Harold, dolefully.

"What rubbish!" growled Alan; "you're *not* going to have them, Harold; you can't till Ethel has had them first herself; you daren't,

you know; don't you recollect what Nurse says
when you want to be helped to pudding before
her,—' Age before honesty, Master Harold ; '
and so Ethel shall have the measles first too ! "

" I wont, Alan," whined Ethel ; " if you say
such horrid things, I'll tell Mamma. I shan't
have the measles, shall I Nurse ? "

" I hope not, from my heart," answered
Nurse, very fervently; " I've handful enough
with you as it is, but goodness forbid you
should be all laid up just now."

Next morning, when Ethel was washed and
dressed, and went into the day nursery to
breakfast, Alan beckoned her out with a very
grave face, and told her to follow him down to
the school-room. She did so, full of curiosity
at the unusual event; but when he opened the
door and led her in, she was still further puzzled.
The tablecloth was laid for breakfast for the
elder ones, but the blinds were all down, and
on the table lay something stretched out under
a towel.

" Take it off and look, Ethel," said Alan ; and
when she did so, she started back in horror, for
there I lay, with my face and throat all covered

DOLLY'S ATTACK OF THE MEASLES.

with bright red round spots. "She has got the measles, Ethel," said Alan, going off into roars of mischievous laughter.

Poor Ethel shrieked and rushed away, sobbing as if her heart would break, till there was such a commotion that Papa came in to see what was the matter. He was very angry indeed with Alan, and told him how cruel it was to frighten a younger child, and a girl too, in this manner; and Alan's explanation that it was only to punish Ethel for teasing little Harold did not make matters better.

"You have no authority to punish any of your brothers and sisters," said Mr. Johnson; "and you have only reduced yourself to the level of Ethel's childish naughtiness by playing a trick very unworthy of you, and that might have led to worse results. Frightening any one is the most cruel sport that exists, and one of the most dangerous. When you fell out of the boat at Barmouth three months ago, Alan, you would have thought it very cruel of me to keep you holding on to the side of the boat, just to laugh at your fright at being so nearly drowned!"

"But Ethel's fright was so silly and unreasonable," muttered Alan.

"So are most alarms, Alan, but they cause the same suffering, and are sometimes as hurtful in their consequences. Don't let me ever hear of any thing of the kind again. You are, I know, very fond of all your brothers and sisters, and would not give them any pain willingly. Now remember, my boy, in future, that a pain of the mind, such as this fright, is infinitely worse than a severe blow, and it is not manly to hurt the weaker ones in any way."

Alan was really sorry for the end of his freak, and he kissed Ethel, and remembered the lesson I have no doubt. But the silly little girl never liked me again, although Nurse washed me white, in her careful way, scrubbing off all the red paint with which Alan had so profusely embellished me. And after a while I had so completely fallen into oblivion, that I was undisturbed, till one evening, some years after, when Ethel was fifteen, and had forgotten all about my early disfigurement, I was fetched out to amuse little Florry Spenser, who drank tea there, and she cuddled me up so tight, and was so loath to part with me, that she was allowed to carry me home, and played with me for some days. My reign, however, did not last very long, for when her aunt gave her a very grand new wax baby, I was cast aside, and have lived here ever since in the deepest seclusion, as you are all aware. And now, my friends, I have done my poor best in your service, and have finished.

And the Doll sank back with a weary sigh.

The Ball, who, by virtue of having been the first story teller, seemed to have taken on himself the office of spokesman, made the Doll an elaborate compliment on her story, and then, as her representative, requested the Toy Kitchen to take up the next story.

CHAPTER VII.

THE TOY KITCHEN; AND ITS MAKER.

WHICH mine, said the Kitchen, will take you, I am afraid, ladies and gentlemen, into a lower class of society than you are used to. I am not much of a hand at telling stories, and can't find words to say what I would, but I'll do my best. My first start in life is very easily described, for I am the handiwork of an old man who lived in a dark underground kitchen in one of the back streets of Westminster. Old Joe's neighbours were not, I am afraid, at all of a respectable kind, setting apart their poverty; but the old man held himself aloof and earned his scanty living, troubling no one, and interfering with none. From all I have heard him mutter to himself in his odd way while he was busy, and from what I heard his only visitor say, I think he must have been a paper-hanger or carpenter.

But he had been disabled from active work by a fall from a window which he was cleaning, and after that, had been sorely put to it, in order to earn a living. I am sure he must have had two little children at some time or other, and no doubt lost them from some of the countless illnesses which lie ready in waiting, like great flocks of wolves, for the *poor* children in great cities. Perhaps the wolf in their case was called " Fever," or perhaps "Cholera"; or, more likely still, "Hunger," or " Want of fresh air"; but all I can tell is that they were both dead since their mother, who must have died and left them all early, and poor old Joe then cared no more to exert himself in seeking the work that was so hard to get, and so difficult to keep.

The business the old man now took up, his trade, as he called it, was the making of little toy kitchens, which he hawked about once a week, and sold for the modest sum of twopence each. They were most ingeniously made out of pieces of very thin board, something of the same kind they make hat boxes of. These pieces he bought in large quantities cheap, and

cut to suit his purpose. The floors were made
of more solid wood, and the walls were papered
with odd scraps of wall paper, sample patterns
and such like, which some of his old employers
gave him. The old man, with a few bits of
wood, and the help of a little rough paint,
constructed the rude likeness of a kitchen range,
and a dresser, and very tidy little affairs we
were for the price.

"I should like to put a kitchen table," said
old Joe, surveying me with a critical eye, half
screwed up; "it would make it more comferble
like, and make both ends match. But I can't
do it for the money no how. I'm bound to
make a penny at least on each one to pay for
my time, so the table must wait till better
days."

I was a larger and better specimen of Joe's
work, for I had been made at a time when the
stock had been rather large, and prices low,
and so I was generally kept as a sort of show
article of what Joe *could* do when he liked.
I had more room than Joe generally measured
out to his usual kitchens, and having been
originally papered with an especially neat and

"becoming" hanging, as Joe said, I had become quite a ruling favourite with the old man. I was now promoted to the place of honour on his tray, not for selling purposes, but for exhibition.

"That there chap will cost fourpence," replied Joe to all his little customers when they picked me out; "leastways one like him. This here, you see, is my adver-*tise*-ment. I couldn't afford to sell one like it for less than fourpence. The walls are so well papered, you see, and the bars of the range is shown, with the flames a rushin through 'em !"

"I should like a nice ittle kishin," said a fat, roley-poley little butcher's daughter to her burly father, as he was leisurely wandering outside his shop, admiring and looking over his nice joints of prime meat.

"Like a what, my duck?" said the jolly butcher, lifting up the rosy little petitioner, and giving her an airy ride on his shoulder; "what is it my pussy cat wants to-day of her dad?"

"A kishin," said the child, "a kishin—old man got such lots of kishins !"

The butcher gazed about him with a calm,

placid, satisfied air, like one of his own slain bullocks, when grazing peacefully in their meadows, and then catching sight of Joe in the distance, ran heavily after him with the delighted child. They soon reached the old man, and turned over his wares.

" There's a booful one, dad," said the fat child, " a booful one with a fire lighted! Oh, I like that *so* much ! "

" I'll bring ye one next week, Miss," replied old Joe, seeing they were good customers; "this here ain't for sale, but I'll bring the fellow to he next week."

" I want it now," pouted the child, peevishly.

" What's the price of him, master?" asked the butcher. " Don't be cross, Phoebe, you shall have it."

" I can't sell he," replied the old man, " but I'll bring you another just like it to-night, and it will be fourpence; I can't sell 'em no lower because of the time and trouble they takes."

" I want it now, I want a kishin now," whined Phoebe, hiding her red, cross face on her father's shoulder.

" I'll give ye sixpence for that one, old chap,"

said her father, positively, "and if you won't sell
it, you may go to Coventry, if you like!"

"I wouldn't sell that one for a shilling for a
reason I have," said Joe; "but as little Miss
have a set her heart on it so, I'll go back and
fetch t'other one now. Will that do, little
Missee? And if you are a good girl, and
don't cry, and wait with patience till I come
back, old Joe will bring you a kitchen table
with it into the bargain!"

Like a sensible child, as she was, Phoebe said
she would, and nodding a half reluctant and
doubting farewell to the old man, she saw him
set off at his best pace on his way home to
fetch her the fellow kitchen to myself. And not
for any sum of money would old Joe have
broken any promise he had made to a child.
When he got back to his dark, cold room, he
found his one friendly visitor waiting for him,
but only begged her to sit down and wait for
him a little while so that he could run back to
the child with the toy. He was more than
rewarded, even in very profitable ways, for not
only did the little girl, who had been eagerly
watching for him on the steps, rush out clap-

ping her hands for the promised Kitchen, but the good-natured butcher, seeing how the old man must have hurried to keep his word to the little one, gave him a nice bit of steak at the same time with the price of the toy, telling him he was afraid he would miss his dinner, and so, perhaps, that would make up.

"Thank ye, kindly," replied the old man, "but you see I ain't no dinner to lose to speak of, cos I always has a crust of bread and cheese, leastways, unless any kind soul gives me a old bone or some broken wittles!"

"Well, you can have a cosy broil to-day," laughed the butcher; "'tis prime meat, and that I'll answer for!"

Poor old Joe trotted off in high glee with his prize, buying a "happorth" of onions and a "pennorth of all sorts" to flavour his stew with. For old Joe, being a handy and sensible sort of fellow, had in course of time become quite a cook, with the poor scraps his scanty means furnished. Nor was he the only one to benefit by it, for many a tea-cupful of what was proudly called "broth" did Joe spare to one or two starving mothers hard by, for their ailing little ones. But old Joe had a visitor to-day, his long lost wife's blind sister, and so he was proud indeed to make a feast in her honour; and while his little scrap of meat was slowly simmering, with the odds and ends of garden-stuff he had bought, Joe made his visitor as comfortable as he could, and gave her his kitchens to "feel," as she could not see.

"I'm getting quite a hand at making 'em, Liza," said the old man, cheerily; "I've got quite a sight of little customers, and I think I shall get on by degrees, you know, werry slow, to make some better-most kinds, and sell the bigger ones at fourpence a-piece! And then I can throw in a kitchen table into the bargain, you know, which will make 'em more completer."

Poor blind Liza admired to his heart's content, and felt us all over with her wonderfully sensitive fingers, which almost seemed to find out what sort of paper we were covered with, and she was not without her bit of proud satisfaction, too, for she had brought Joe a pretty little square basket, with a lid to it, which had been the work of her own poor, unguided fingers. She had been placed by a very charitable lady in a blind school, where she had learned basket-work, and she now was able to help her old mother by her work, which was disposed of for her at a shop established for that especial purpose in the Euston Road.

Joe was mightily delighted with his basket, and said it was what he had been wanting all along to keep his coppers in on his tray of toys. And so, after a merry evening, Joe limped off to see the poor blind woman safe to her home, about three miles distant. This was old Joe's solitary holiday for many a month, for he had no friends and few acquaintances, except the poor women who came thankfully to him now and then for one of his savoury messes for their sick little ones, and they had no time to spare, for they were most of them poor hardworking drudges, who were very grateful for his help, and indeed often brought him their own poor scraps of food to cook for their little invalids, while they earned a few pence by washing, or hawking flowers, or fire papers. And the kind-hearted old man would stir and simmer the scanty scraps in his solitary saucepan, and take a world of care and pains with the " broth " to make it relishing for the poor sickly little babes. He would often put it into the cracked mug or pie-dish, and carry it himself to the forlorn sufferer, and stay and have a bit of merry chat. There was not a child in the neighbourhood who did not know and love Joe, and few indeed who had not received some small kindness from him. He was only a very poor and infirm old man, and had but little in his power to give or do, but what he could was all done so cheerfully and kindly, that the very sight of his old wrinkled, weather-beaten face seemed like sunshine in the wretched rooms where poverty and want lived so hardly.

More than one even of his little kitchens had been generously given away by Joe, and though they were really of no value, to him they were the produce of hours of labour and pains, and the means by which he earned his scanty living. Poor little Biddy Doolan, a small child, who had been wasting away many months in a slow decline, was found by her mother (who had gone to the dispensary for some medicine for her), lying back on the heap of straw, cold and lifeless, with the treasured kitchen, the *one* toy of a long miserable childhood, cuddled fast in the thin stiff arms. Old Joe cried over her like a child, and was more active than ever in his errands among the sick children. He was at last christened "Dr. Joe," by universal consent, and was really often sent for after the regular doctor, and he came as regularly, although he had no fee beyond the thanks of his poor little patients.

I used always to accompany him in his weekly long journeys, holding the place of honour on the trays, next to Liza's basket, and many a funny scene have we witnessed together. Joe's customers were "legion," for every child that could raise twopence was ready enough to buy one of the kitchens. And as times did get a little better, Joe *was* able to add the long wished-for wooden table, which gave a great finish and air of reality to his little constructions. His sales rose one third after this, and Joe's spirits went up with them. On Liza's next visit she suggested that he might make a parlour too, she thought, and old Joe, getting quite venture-some, jumped at the idea.

"I've a cousin in service, Joe," said Liza,

"she lives nurse at Mrs. Spencer's, and I'll ask her if she can't save us up a few bits and scraps of print and muslin. I think I could help you a little too, even if 'tis only in a small way."

"Thankee sure, Liza," replied Joe, delighted, "and now I'll tell ye what, you and mother come up some afternoon, and we'll see what we can do between us all. I'll see ye safe back at night."

And blind Liza and her mother did come, and what between Liza's neat and clever fingers, her old mother's sharp eyes, and Joe's own handy work, they had speedily turned out half a dozen little parlours, that Joe fairly hopped round, shouting with delight. The cousin had been very generous and set them up with a tolerable hoard of bits and scraps, so that, what with paper and paint and all, they were, as Joe declared, "fit for a queen to live in." The walls were papered with Joe's choicest scraps, and the floor carpeted with a piece of print, while scraps of muslin stood for curtains. Liza had manufactured some square cushions of a suitable size, which did duty for ottomans, and a round piece of card board, glued on a pillar leg, composed of an empty cotton reel painted brown, did duty for a centre table. Then Joe decorated the centre of the back wall with what he considered a splendid likeness of a grand drawing room grate. He looked at his work with great satisfaction, and was never weary of pointing out the best charms of each parlour to the old lady, Liza's mother, who really was a very useful and agreeable helper to the party. She perched her old horn spectacles on the tip of her little nose, and peeped in, suggesting improvements here and there, and she cut out the carpets quite tidily. Their only regret was that Liza could not see them too, but she was so cheerful, and guessed and described what the parlours were like so well, that they declared she must have eyes in the tips of her fingers.

"Now," said Joe, as they finished the sixth by the dim light of a halfpenny dip, "ladies, I'm uncommon obliged to you for your help, which great it is, and well I shall do by it, I don't doubt, but I'm afraid I shan't manage 'em so well for myself arterwards."

"O yes, you will Joe," replied Liza, cheerfully; "you know you always were a handy man ; you can cut the carpets and curtains every bit as well as mother can. And as for the ottomy's, I'll make you a dozen or two when I'm home, and I'll bring 'em to you next week, or what's better still, you can fetch 'em. Don't you think its Joe's turn to return our visit, mother?"

"Indeed I do," replied the old woman, "and Joseph knows he'll be welcome."

And thus it was arranged, and in about ten days' time Joe went to their house, and carried them a very glowing account of the remarkable success that had attended him "along of the parlours;" he also opened his heart so much, that he actually took me with him, as an offering to Liza. I am very much afraid the glory of those horrid little new parlours had quite put him out of conceit with me. Liza had been as good as her word, and furnished Joe with a pocket full of ottomy's, all covered with gay shreds of chintz. The nurse at Mrs. Spencer's had sent them a most bountiful collection of bits, for she had spoken to her mistress, and told her the purpose she was collecting them for, and Mrs. Spenser, with her usual kindness, had herself found a good parcel of bits to add to the store.

On hearing this, Joe thought he could do no less than to leave me with his humble and grateful duty to the young ladies at Mrs. Spenser's house, on his way back to his own underground home. And so this is how I became a member of your circle, my friends, and have had the honour of being called on to amuse you in my turn. I believe, from a few words I heard nurse let fall some time ago, that my old master is still alive, and doing a flourishing trade in "Kitchens and Parlours!" And I have no doubt he is still carrying out his less lucrative, but charitable calling, among the sick children of his wretched neighbourhood.

"We are all much obliged to you for your history," said the Ball, "which is quite as interesting as any we have heard this evening. And now I shall call upon our very fair friend the Shuttlecock for the next story."

CHAPTER VIII.

THE FATE OF THE SHUTTLECOCK.

"OH," simpered the Shuttlecock, "I am quite distracted at the idea of being called upon to take any part in public affairs. And, alas, how it will torture my sensitive feelings to recall to mind the bright scenes in which I appeared, and was once one of the most important actors! Ah, my friends, although you see me reduced to this—to *this* miserable shadow of what I once was—you are not to imagine I was always thus faded, thus broken and destroyed! No! In my youth my heart was indeed light within me ; for was it not of the best and most expensive species of cork ? A portion of a noble tree that once waved its umbrageous branches in the fair land of Spain, and that fulfilled a better purpose, even than that of sheltering a fair

I

group of dark-eyed Castilian maids, by furnishing the substance that was to assume so fair a shape as I did once! My outside was no less beautiful, for I was covered with the best and brightest hued scarlet morocco leather, and gilded richly besides. A noble coronet of graceful plumes, once white as driven snow, adorned me, plucked I doubt not, from the soaring pinion of some beautiful bird. Not low, therefore, could have been the rank of him to whom I owe my existence; indeed I have very little reason to doubt that he was of very ancient lineage and noble name. But alas! It is unavailing to recall all these bright departed glories, which have long, long since fled, and left me the wreck you behold me!"

So saying, the Shuttlecock feebly waved her last remaining dingy feather, and sank down on her side, as if in despair. But the Kite fanned her very busily; and the Humming Top gave her such a long, tiresome lecture on the duty of being contented, that she speedily recovered herself, and continued her story.

My first public appearance in life was on the occasion of a superb Fancy Fair, which was held in the ancestral park of one of our country's proudest nobles. It was for the benefit of a distinguished charity, and some of the fairest and most fashionable ladies of the court were to hold stalls on the occasion. It was whispered that even Royalty or some of its branches might visit the spot, and therefore every effort was made to give the fête a worthy success. Words would fail me were I to describe to you the beauty of the scene on the important day. A monster marquee was erected on the most commanding site in the fine domain, and decorated gaily with the flags of all nations. A fine avenue of aged trees made a noble sheltered walk for the gay visitors, and it led almost all the way to the marquee, the space between being covered with a smart scarlet-striped awning overhead.

I had time to observe all this, as I was carried in a basket from the Castle, down the green slopes to the marquee, by one of the many smart ladies' maids in attendance. But when we entered, the effect, at once so fairy-like and so elegant, rendered me motionless and almost senseless. The interior was draped with pink and green, and the elegant stalls were being laid out with all their pretty trifles. I was honoured with a place on the stall of the Duchess herself, and had therefore an excellent opportunity of witnessing the habits and manners of real high life, and I felt at once in my element. Here, thought I, am I placed in my natural sphere, a dweller with the fair and the noble, surrounded with rank and beauty, and breathing only the refined air of higher life. I was cut short in my musings by Lord Adolphus, the youngest son of the Duchess, who, with the charming vivacity so natural to his birth and station, abstracted me from the dainty basket in which I reposed, with a few companions of less merit. I was soon in full activity, and took my first flights to admiration, by the ready and graceful assistance of himself and a young companion, also a titled member of society.

" What a jolly shuttlecock," remarked Lord Adolphus, " it goes as high as the top of the tent, I declare. I say, Gerry, do you think you could pitch it over, outside ? I'll bet you two-pence you don't."

" I'll lay six to one, I *do*," replied Sir Gerald,

running eagerly out of the tent, with me in his hand. He did not exhibit *quite* the same amount of refinement as his noble young friend; in fact, he was more like boys in general, and lacked that *perfume*, if I may call it so, of high breeding which so signally showed itself in *my* earliest friend, Lord Adolphus. After a spirited contest between the two gallant boys, I *was* thrown over the marquee, and, after such a lofty and prolonged flight, fell exhausted, without the power of saving myself, into a little crystal pool of water close by. I heard my noble young playfellows searching for me everywhere, and began to entertain a deadly fear that I should be left in my watery prison. Luckily, the warm day and their game had made them thirsty, and they both came to quench their thirst here, little thinking of finding me, whom they had no doubt so long and vainly searched for.

"By Jove, Dolly," cried Sir Gerald, "*here's* the shuttlecock after all!"

"What a lark," replied Lord Adolphus; "it's been chucked into old Rosamond's well, and ought to come out beautiful for ever!"

"I'm glad we found it," said Sir Gerald;

"or perhaps there'd have been a row. I saw
Githa count 'em all, and she'd have been sure
to bully us about it."

"We could have given her the tin for it
then," replied Adolphus, "only I'm so hard
up just now. I owe a lot of money for sweets
and tarts; and I want to buy a cricket bat this
quarter. But hulloa, Gerry, how wet the
beggar is?"

But the dear gentlemanly fellow, soon reme-
died this fault, for he wiped me carefully with
his own cambric handkerchief, and I was not
the worse, except that my coronet of plumes
looked rather damp, or, as Sir Gerald facetiously
expressed it, "all draggletail!"

A little sojourn in the glowing Sun, soon
restored my feathers to their early beauty, as
I was carefully taken back, no worse for my
pleasant little gambol, and placed in the basket
again, on the Duchess's stall. The hour of
opening arrived, one o'clock; but, out upon the
cruel Fates! long before the turning point of
noon, lowering clouds had veiled the bright,
too treacherously bright rays of the Sun, and
heavy, drenching showers succeeded, ending in

a steady downpour that promised to last out the day. Oh dear! What ruin and destruction ensued to the elegant erection of the morning! The marquee leaked in many places from the sudden violence of the storm, and none of the precautions, hastily taken, would make it quite water-tight. The unlucky visitors, with their gay summer dresses all sopped and clinging with wet, crowded in to gain what little shelter they could; and all was damp, dreary and desolate! The higher class, more fortunate than the rest, accompanied the Duchess to the Castle; the stalls were deserted in favour of the younger, and less particular among the gay party, and the marquee was only crowded by the more persevering vulgar mob, who were determined to have, as I heard one of the horrors avow, "their full penn'orth," all they could see and get for their money.

An evil destiny which seems to have fallen upon me early, relentlessly followed me now, and ruled my unwilling sacrifice. I was positively sold from the stall of the Duchess, by her Grace's own maid, to a rich grocer in the city, for the sum of sixpence! Oh, degradation indeed! Fallen, fallen, fallen from my high estate indeed was I. No friendly hand interposed; no better purchaser came, so I was ignominiously wrapped in paper and put in Mr. Figge's pocket. Nor had ruthless fortune yet done with me, for when I was carried to the abode of the Figge's, although I had been really destined as a gift to his only daughter, Araminta Philippina, I was, by mistake in the hurry of returning, dropped in the carriage, and although a vigorous search seemed to be made by the fine footman, he did not succeed in finding me, and I remained hid in a far back corner of the roomy equipage for some days. Had I fallen to the share of Araminta Philippina, I should at least have retained the small consolation of being incessantly pointed out as having been bought from the Duchess herself, and a faint ray of my lost station would have still glimmered about me.

But, alas, on emerging from my obscurity, I found I had indeed fallen in life, and from the highest to the lowest, for I was now located in the Mews, where Mr. Figge's carriage was kept; and having been found during its dusting and arrangement by the wife of the coachman, I was handed over to her horrible tribe of uncouth, ill-behaved children.

Oh, for the language that I heard round me now! It made my very feathers quiver sometimes; and as for the flights I took now, —ugh—it makes me shudder to recall them! I who had bathed in fair Rosamond's crystal stream, was now doomed to be plunged in the inky rills that ran in the gutters round the sooty roofs. My beautiful red leather cover was soon dyed a dingy black; most of my feathers were violently pulled out by some of the younger ones, and the rest became somewhat of the colour of a London sparrow. At last, as a sort of release from worse miseries, I was tossed up so high by the horrid little flat wooden bat, which now became the means of my ascending, (and that in the hands of the coachman's eldest son, was an instrument of indiscriminate torment to everything animate and inanimate), that I fell on the ledge of a back window in one of the houses in a square adjoining. The boy, I imagine, did not dare to go round to the house to ask for me again, and

was therefore reduced to his original stock of
playthings, consisting chiefly of a mutilated
ginger-beer bottle, some oyster shells, and a
brickbat.

Meanwhile I dwelt for some time on the
window ledge, exposed to the wind and rain,
but at any rate free from the vulgar annoyances
to which I had been subjected of late. And this
I could endure more calmly, and I had almost
become resigned to my hard lot, when one day
to my astonishment the window was opened. A
young woman leant out with a hammer and
nails in her hands, and proceeded to fix one in
firmly on the side of the window. She did not
see me, for I had become securely lodged in the
other corner almost out of sight, and so she did
not either pick me up, nor what I secretly feared
most, throw me back again into the low haunts
of my former miserable and odious life. She
contented herself with merely hanging out a
bird in its cage, and then partially closed the
window again, and, I suppose, left the room.

It is not my usual habit to make acquaintance
too readily with strangers, and therefore I did
not commence a conversation with my feathered

neighbour; but, then, as you are doubtless well aware, birds are generally of a sociable disposition, and prone to make remarks and enter into conversation with comparative strangers. And my new neighbour proved no exception to the rule, for he began to chatter and chirp in the most voluble manner, and had speedily related all his own personal history, and that of several members of his family. But I am not very fond of the affairs of people that do not belong to my own class, and therefore did not pay much attention to his gossip. He was of a prying disposition too, as very communicative people generally are, and seemed rather anxious to know all about me. But I rather politely but loftily repelled him, for I did not choose my misfortunes to be the common talk of such small people. So I briefly informed him I had been far better off, and indeed it was now, only owing to peculiar circumstances I wished to remain for a time in comparative retirement.

From him I learned that his owner was the under housemaid at this house, and that she was shortly about to leave, having obtained another situation where there was less work to do.

The bird prattled in a lively fashion about the
merry life he had led hitherto and the continued change he had seen, and seemed to be
quite looking forward to what he called " his
next place."

" I only wish you were going with me, you
poor thing; I am sure you must be moped to
death with staying up here by yourself so long.
Don't you think you could manage to roll into
my cage, and then we could go off together? "

My propriety was terribly shocked by this
proposal of the goldfinch's, and for some time I
could give him no answer.

" You silly thing ! " said he, angrily, at last,
" surely you may travel with your own relations,
and you know you and I must be kin, because
we have both the distinguished ornament of
feathers."

This delicate compliment softened me a little,
I must confess ! " said the Shuttlecock, bridling
up with a very dignified air, which, in her
dilapidated state, with her one ragged feather
sticking out all awry, was a very comic affair.
Consequently none of the toys could help
laughing; as for the Kite, he was so amused that

he waggled about like a sail in a rough wind. Even the languid, delicate Doll could not forbear a feeble smile, and the Shuttlecock became so indignant, that she would have bounced out of the party, had her powers been equal to her spirit. But, alas, though her cork was still sound, her wings had departed, and the solitary draggletail feather was not sufficient to waft her above the rude mirth of her auditors. But she was so deeply offended that it took the Ball a long time, and a world of trouble, to pacify her. At last, on his hinting that as time was passing by he should be reduced to calling upon another member present for a story, she permitted herself to be pacified, and resumed her narrative, with a more haughty air, and in finer words than before:—

" My poor autobiography can be concluded in very few words now, for I have but little more to relate. My feathered connection, for he certainly made his claim good to a distant relationship, would take no denial, and told me he had set his heart on taking me with him when he went; and that he had a plan of his own by which he would be able to carry out his purpose. I therefore submitted to his decision, and counted the days, I must honestly own, very eagerly, until the period of our joint captivity arrived. The evening before, my bird relation requested a friendly Breeze, with whom he was on friendly terms, to blow me close to his cage. I was then, I should tell you, possessed still of several of my plumes, although they were in a dingy condition, and therefore more able to help myself. A good strong gust then, at the right moment, and carefully adjusted to the right quarter, sufficed to take me to the ledge of the bird's food box. From thence he speedily, though with some amount of hard work, managed to pull and drag me inside the cage, a friendly wire stretching widely for the purpose. My friend then carefully pushed me under his seed-box, knowing that as long as I was pretty well out of sight, his mistress, Mary, would not take much trouble about it. From former experience and frequent removes, he knew well she would only find time to tie him up, cage and all, in a blue handkerchief, and carry him off at the very last moment. All this came to pass, as he so sagely predicted, and after being blinded-up in this fashion for some time, and jogged and shaken in a very uncomfortable manner, we came to our journey's end in a bedroom in this house. We were not disturbed till next morning, for Mary had only time to give my friend his seed and water, before she set off on her new round of duties. Two days after, however, she managed to find time to think of the bird.

"You shall go down stairs into the kitchen, my pretty Dick," said she, chirping to him, "for cook says she is fond of birds, and will give me some sugar for you. But I must clean your cage first, for you are not fit to be seen, I'm sure, now!"

And so saying, she proceeded to make Dick's house clean and neat, and in the course of doing so, she came upon me. "Why, Dickey," she said, laughing, "have you been trying a game of shuttlecock, by way of sport? How came this in your cage, I wonder!"

Dick tried to explain in his bird fashion, and did so, *I* thought, very intelligibly, but, then, as you know, all human beings are so very difficult of comprehension. So she took me out in spite of all my poor cousin's protests, and laid me on the table in her room. On the following Sunday, when Mary was to stay at home with the little ones while nurse went to church, she remembered me, and brought me down to amuse the young Spensers. Like all the rest of their race, they soon became tired of me, and I was thrust away in this dusty cupboard till now. Of all the histories that have been related to amuse you, none, I am sure, have surpassed mine for vicissitudes and changes. I was the early companion of Duchesses and Lords, and yet have been doomed to endure the society of coachmen and stable boys, and to be rescued from a rackety bird-cage to end my days in a dusty cupboard !

Then the Shuttlecock ceased to speak, and betook herself to her corner, to bewail in private the sad downfall she had endured.

"And now," said the Ball, "I will call upon our venerable friend, the Noah's Ark; I am sure he will be able to tell us a great deal that is very interesting about himself and his numerous tribe."

The poor old Ark creaked slowly forward, and announced his willingness to add his history to the rest, beginning in the following words.

CHAPTER IX.

WHAT BECAME OF NOAH'S ARK AND ALL ITS BEASTS.

I MUST tell you a little about the hands that first made us, and to do so I must take you in fancy to the high Alps in Switzerland. There, during the long bright summer months, according to the practice of the country, the flocks and herds are pastured, only descending to the villages in autumn, when food and fodder grow scant. A temporary dwelling is erected, in which the Sennerin, the young girl who usually takes charge of them, lives for the season, and where she follows the dairy business peculiar to her calling. The long summer days pass so calmly and pleasantly there, while the cows and their young ones crop the juicy herbage of these mountain pastures. Meanwhile the shepherd lads, and those who are not busied in more active labours, often pass their leisure hours, while guarding their flocks with the help of their intelligent dogs, in carving cleverly some pretty little toys in the light wood peculiar to their province. These find a ready sale with the travellers, who climb these lofty heights to feast their eyes on the ranges of distant peaks and Alpine passes, that seem almost reaching up to the sky.

Sitting on the grass, with their quaint, old-fashioned knives, these lads carve elegant and graceful trifles, that often eventually find their way into royal palaces, and are used by many dainty fingers. My maker, however, was more given to the construction of toys for children; he preferred fashioning all kinds of animals and reptiles, to making flower bestudded paper knives or perforated work baskets; and he found a very good and ready sale for all he had time to manufacture. By his patient and incessant industry, he had earned a comfortable living for many years for his blind and aged mother, to whom he was a most dutiful and tender son. Never a penny of Fritz's money was spent in idle folly, for neither gay ribbons for his hat nor silver buckles for his shoes ever wiled away his earned money from its pious purpose. He certainly was a true but very humble admirer of our Sennerin, who was the only daughter of a rich farmer of the village; and I had a few opportunities for noticing that she always prized more the simple Alpine roses, for which Fritz had climbed many a dangerous spot, than she did the elaborate carvings or purchased trinkets which were offered to her by others. I hope long ere this, Fritz, the good son and industrious villager, is the owner of the goodly farm, and the happy husband of the pretty Sennerin. But I did not remain long enough to know much of the progress of his affairs; for although it took him half the summer to make me and two similar Arks, we were readily disposed of at once, on his return to the village. The toy merchant made his yearly visit then, and carried us all off with a host of other articles of similar manufacture.

I hope I may be excused for a little pardon-able vanity in describing our personal appear-ance to you; for, in common with you all, I have been also divested by time and rough usage of most of my early charms. When I was first springing from beneath the skilful fingers of Fritz, I was the prettiest specimen of a model Swiss cottage set upon a boat floor, that ever was made. My walls were formed of the pretty very white species of wood, used by these deft shepherd carvers, and light, graceful openwork patterns were formed on them, by delicately cut cross pieces of a darker shade. The roof, with wide projecting eaves, after the regular châlet pattern, had its cross beams, and here and there the usual stones, laid on it, which, in the original structures, are placed there to add some weight of resistance to the furious mountain gales that come sweeping down the deep gorges. There was a row of windows, which were really cut out and glazed, through which you might obtain a view of the jumble of animals huddled together inside. A perforated gallery of light wood ran all round the walls half way up, from whence a staircase, general to these Swiss cottages, led down, and in this case terminated on the floor of the flat wooden boat, which of rather unusual depth, formed the bottom of the Ark.

As to my contents, they were of a rather miscellaneous character, for although Fritz had

a natural love for animals, and considerable
success in copying those with which he was
acquainted, his knowledge of the more distant
creation was limited to the quaint old woodcuts
in his mother's Bible, in which they were drawn
with more spirit and imagination than correct-
ness.   And so Fritz's horses, oxen, pigs, sheep,
dogs, and goats were characteristic and good,
but his elephant and camel, though original,
were eccentric, to use a mild term.   They were
all executed, however, with great pains, and the
wood from which they were carved was specially
selected with a view to their colour and marks.
Thus, for example, the tiger, though his outline
and shape were rather doubtful, and he partook
more than he should of the square frame of a
cow, was cut out of a bit of wood where a knot
had been, which caused it to be streaked in a
manner very suitable to the stripes of that
animal.   The birds generally were a greater success, for with most of these Fritz was tolerably
familiar.   We had certainly all spent a very
pleasant summer, high up in the Alps, with the
most delicious clear sky overhead and the fra-
grant herbage beneath.   It was so calm and clear,

that the silence.was broken alone by the far
off sheep and goat bells, the faint low of the
drowsy cattle, or the sweet song of distant birds.
How often I have recalled that pleasant early
life, which was so very speedily terminated.

The toy merchant soon packed up his wares
and departed, and we saw and heard nothing
more, until we were unpacked from a huge case
of other toys, and placed in the window of a
famous toyshop in St. Paul's Churchyard.   In
the window there, for some months, we attracted
numberless groups of delighted little admirers,
but our high price placed us beyond the reach
of most people.   Our turn came at last; we
were selected by a doating grandpapa for his
pet little grand-daughter, and carefully packed
up and taken to the abode of our future owner.
The pretty little child was too young as yet to
have such a beautiful and costly toy in her own
charge, so her Mamma undertook the care of
us. and Beatrice was allowed to play with us
occasionally.

She was a queer little mortal, this new
mistress of ours, and not particularly fond of
toys in general.   She was highly delighted at

first, and twice or thrice when she was allowed to play with us, she arranged us carefully in pairs on the table. But when Nurse or Mamma tried to improve her knowledge, and give her a sly object lesson on zoology, Miss Beatrice grew refractory, and cared for us no more. Unfortunately on one occasion when her Mamma was seriously ill, the nurse gave us to her to play with, to keep her quiet, and the whole house being somewhat upset by the illness, the child was not taken much notice of. Alas, when Nurse came in the evening to collect my animals and put me away, she found a most deplorable state of things. Beatrice had been dragging me about as a carriage for her doll, and had thus damaged my pretty railed gallery and staircase past all mending. My roof was in three pieces, and the reckless little savage had first strewn all my beasts over the floor, and then as deliberately walked over them. Oh, what a havoc was there! My poor dear cows and sheep, that had cost the ingenious Fritz so much time and trouble, had not three legs to boast of between them, and as for the birds, they were most of them pounded to pieces and bits.

I thought with bitter regret of the green mountain heights where we had so merrily proceeded under Fritz's laborious fingers, and had been the admiration of the whole little Swiss village.

When Beatrice's mother was better, she was much vexed to hear what had happened to us, and was very angry indeed with Beatrice for her wilful mischief. I believe from that time, the child took a dislike to us, for she was a capricious, odd-tempered little thing, and certainly never played with us without doing us some further injury. As for the animals, they were left and dropped all over the house. Poor old Grandmamma coming to spend the day, fell down and sprained her ancle by treading on the elephant. The camel was thrown through one of the windows by a little boy visitor during a romp with Beatrice, and Aunt Priscilla was almost irreparably offended the last time she stayed there, by finding a wooden pig in her fur-lined slipper. She put her foot hastily in without seeing it, and hurt it so, that she declared she was lame for a month afterwards. In short, we were always in trouble in some way or other, and Beatrice's mother more than once threatened to give us away.

It would have been a small consolation to us if our young owner had played with us sometimes, or taken ever so little pride in us. But no; she only took us out to bring more shame and disgrace on us, and on herself. For instance, once when her Godmother took her to church for the first time, Beatrice took her handkerchief out of her pocket, and with it a number of wooden animals, which fell in a pattering shower on the pavement. Naughty Beatrice would stop in the middle of the aisle and pick us all up, to the astonishment of the congregation, the horror of her Godmother, and the utter scandal of the grave old clerk. Nay, worse even, for when the sermon commenced, she rushed out of her seat, and began to hunt about under the people's feet in the free benches for a missing camelopard!

After this terrible mishap, Nurse laid hands on all the stray animals she could find, and clapped them all hastily into my box, shutting down the lid decidedly, and promising Beatrice she should see us no more. She was as good as her word, and hid us behind a great pile of clean dimity curtains in the linen closet, where we remained snugly packed away for some time. But, alas! one day our mischievous little mistress, during one of her prowls, chanced to see the open door of the linen closet, and could not resist a sudden raid upon it. To her great joy, she found us, and carefully lugging us out, she hid us in her little cot till bedtime.

It happened to be the day of a dinner party, and all the servants were very busy with the preparations for it, while the lady of the house was equally engaged in superintending the arrangements. In the evening, while dinner was proceeding, Beatrice, well-dressed for the occasion, was taken down into the drawing-room, to wait till she could go in to dessert. Her nurse, no doubt, was using her ears and eyes in other matters, and so the mischievous little maid was left to her own devices. The results, however, were very unpleasantly visible to her Mamma, when having helped a lady to some trifle, she observed her become very red, and lay down her spoon. On enquiry, she found that she had met with a wooden frog in the trifle, and on further search, some more of my unlucky animals were found located among the sweet dishes. A huge dog was floundering in the jelly, and a regular flight of birds had got about the blancmange.

The end of this disagreeable affair was, that Miss Beatrice was sent to bed in dire disgrace, and the poor innocent animals, all sticky from their sweet bath, were consigned to the fire. The few remaining creatures that were left of all the numerous flock Fritz had so proudly made, were hastily gathered together, and with me, given away next morning.

Our next owner was a little boy, a very quiet little fellow, to whom we became the greatest treasure in the world. He thought me the most beautiful toy that was ever made, although I was in such a sadly damaged condition. His only grief was, that my stock of animals had now dwindled down to about twenty, and of these, most were maimed or deficient in some way. However, he wisely made the best of a bad matter, and set to work to repair the damage as well as he could. With his elder brother's kind help, and the loan of a glue-pot, he repaired, as neatly as possible, the breakage of my gallery and staircase. With pins, cork, and sealing-wax, he next proceeded to tinker-up the poor mutilated animals, and succeeded in making them all stand pretty firmly once more. It would have done Fritz's honest heart good to see how carefully the little fellow handled his masterpiece, and how very conscientiously he tried to put all to rights again. And if the horse *had* two odd scarlet legs made out of sealing-wax, it was better than going a cripple for life; and as for the squirrel, he need not have grumbled, for a black pin for a tail was better than none. To be sure, he did stick the bear's head on the wrong way, but then it did not much matter, it only looked as if he had met with a tree he wanted to climb, and was looking up it.

And so once more we were patched up into ordinary respectability, and so pretty did we look, even in our less bright condition, that at last, as Harry was a little too old to play with such toys, and cared much more for making and mending them, we were laid out in great style, and to as much advantage, on the little chess table in the bow window, and covered with a glass shade to preserve us from the dust!

Here we dwelt in state for some years, while

Harry grew up and went to school, and after that to college, and ceased to care for such trifles. And then his mother gave us to Celia Spenser, on her birthday, who was much delighted, and for a long while we were a very favourite toy of hers; but her little brothers and sister made fresh ravages on our impaired value, although it is but fair to say the misfortunes were unintentional, and they were really sorry when they had broken any of my beams, or lost an animal. And now our turn has come to be cast aside, and so here we are with the rest of the old pensioners!

And having said this, the Ark creaked his lid down again, and finished his story, for which he received the thanks of all the assembled party.

"Now," said the Ball, musing gravely, "I shall call next in order on the Marbles to relate their general history, and as I don't know which of them to ask first, I must call upon them collectively."

CHAPTER X.

THE MARBLES AND THEIR PROCEEDINGS.

"WE are of what may be styled republican principles," said a large China Marble, rolling out of the heap. "Of all the speakers who have already come forward, the Kite, Doll, and yourself, for instance, are simple individuals. The Tea-things are a large family, under the rule of their mother, the Tea-pot; a kind of domestic despotism. The Noah's Ark might represent a constitutional or limited monarchy, where the Ark is a sort of governing or holding together of the rest of the members. And so they have all very properly, as representatives, related their own peculiar history. But *we* Marbles are a republic, and therefore can't quite tell all our story as one, because several kinds or classes of us wish to tell their own separate tale."

"I daresay this is all very clever, and very

true," replied the Ball, suppressing a yawn; "but I don't quite understand all you have said. However, let that pass; the only question before us is, how the proceedings are to be arranged in this manner. I think, as President of our party, I can hardly allow all of you to relate a distinct story, because there are several other people who are waiting in their turn, and it is due to them, as well as fair to the rest, not forgetting those who have gone before, that we should not spend all our time in hearing separately half a dozen members of your party."

"But we have no story to tell as a body," urged a Bright Glass Marble; "if you won't hear us separately, we have no whole adventure to relate worth mentioning."

The Ball, somewhat puzzled, consulted gravely with the rest; and after whispering in one corner with the Kite, and in another with the Rocking Horse—after having failed in obtaining any opinion from the Doll, who was too languid to care much about the matter, and having skilfully evaded the Humming Top, who had more to say on the subject than any one cared to hear—he once more took his place, and gave his decision thus:—

"After a consultation and council with several distinguished members of our party, I am happy to tell you that we are willing to allow three of you to relate your separate stories, on the distinct understanding that they do not exceed, in their united length, the narrations that have gone before."

On behalf of his companions, the China Marble who had first spoken, willingly agreed to the terms, and called upon the Bright Glass Marble to speak first. And so the small green glassy thing rolled smoothly forward, looking like a little curled-up snake, and began to speak.

"I am not going to relate to you the usual pursuits and habits of a common Marble! I am not made like them of mere earth or clay, but of glass—bright shining glass—the result of a marvellous combination of different things by the aid of chemical skill and knowledge. These delicate threads that you can perceive winding gracefully and symmetrically through me are of Venetian origin, and the mode of making them—once a trade secret—was first discovered in that "city of an hundred isles."

I was not baked in a hot oven, as my humbler brethren are, but melted and cleared again and again in a far fiercer heat, until my nature became refined and purified, and my clear colour green as the sea which glides like a glittering network through and round Venice.

Nor was all this trouble taken with me only that I might become a mere child's toy, like these dingy, earthen globes; no! I was designed to become a member of a charming party, who lived in separate apartments, on a large mahogany board, and our party was elegantly called for that reason by the French name of *Solitaire!* Some of my family were crimson, some blue, some striped like sea-shells, some flaked with gold, but all beautiful. We lived for a long time appropriately enough in the Crystal Palace, where we lay with hosts of other brilliant things, too numerous to mention, on a long counter in the Bohemian Court. I may say, without vanity, that we were the objects of admiration to thousands, and many of our sparkling host were carried off like trophies, to adorn the mansions of the great and noble.

My destination was at first a fortunate one;

L

but, alas, in common with yourselves, *I* have also met with reverses in life; and on *me*, poor little me, Fate seems to have poured out all her hardest punishment. We were purchased at first by Lord Latimer for his little daughter Florine, and for a while laid on inlaid tables and were only handled by fair and jewelled fingers. I need not enter into the plan of the game of Solitaire, which had just then come out fresh, and was universally popular, for, as in many other cases what is *play* to others is *work* to us. I had nothing to complain of, however, for my fair young mistress was very gentle and lady-like, and skilled in the game, so that we were daintily used and carefully kept. Indeed while we breathed the perfumed air of that luxurious boudoir, sweetened with the rarest exotic flowers, and ornamented with every graceful trinket and toy that could please its owner, our life passed like a fairy dream. But sweet and amiable as Florine was, she too had her faults, and a love of change and novelty was one of them. When she had possessed us a brief year, she grew weary of us, and passed on to other amusements. Her whole thoughts were now given to table croquet, and we lay idle and disused. At last one day we were coolly given away to little Rosie Herbert, a small friend of hers, who carried us exultingly off at once. Unluckily our new owner was a mere raw school girl, and having no mother, and more of her own way than was good for her, we were taken by her to school, and there we ran the gauntlet of twenty or thirty school girls, and never knew ten minutes' peace through the day, except at meal times. We now became acquainted with rough treatment, for we were usually sent rolling on the floor into all corners of the room half a dozen times a day, and many of my friends were lost entirely by these means. What became of them eventually I do not know, as we never met all together again, the vacant place in the board being filled up by Rosie with *beans*, neighbours, I need hardly say, not by any means acceptable to the poor remainder of us! What we underwent at that dreadful school, or even a tithe of the mischievous pranks we saw there, would take too long a time to describe; and the only wonder is, that any of us escaped to tell the tale, for when our novelty wore off, the value for us lessened also. One unscrupulous girl made frequent use of us to torment her enemies by putting some of us in their beds, others in their shoes, nay, even one girl narrowly escaped choking by nearly swallowing *me* in a cup of tea, into which I had been slily slipped. One or two of us broke a few window panes, and we were frequently sent rolling about the writing table, until at last Miss Blunt desired Rosie to collect us all, and keep us in her play-box till the holidays, on pain of entire confiscation.

We then, or at least the few survivors of our once numerous band, hoped we had now at last a little interval of peace, before we retired into private life. On once more emerging from obscurity, and accompanying Rosie home, we found that our chance was not much improved, for we were continually being slily purloined to replenish her brother Robert's marble bag. For a long time I had seen my companions gradually disappearing one by one, and dreaded the time when I too must follow, and at last the terrible moment arrived. I was carried off, and once more became a haunter of a school, but this time it was one for boys, and from my former experience, I was in utter despair at the fate before me. Fortunately, however, in the first game of marbles in which Robert indulged after I came into his possession, I was won by Frank Spenser. He was just on the eve of leaving school, and consequently I had no very unpleasant encounters to anticipate. With the rest of my companions I was put aside and forgotten, and that is how I came to reside in the toy cupboard!"

"Well," said one of the common marbles, coming forward, "I can't lay any claim to such a fine appearance, nor shall I be able to relate such a distinguished history. My origin is humble enough, for I am made of clay, in common with many other things of far more importance than marbles. My first appearance in life was in a wicker basket with a lot of others in the dingy window of old Spattleberry's shop, where we lived in company with bottles of lollipops, ginger beer, jam tarts, string, slate-pencil, tops, knives, and parliament. I have lived in a public school almost all my life, and I only wish I could get back there once more. None of your grand scented drawing rooms and faddling girls for me! I prefer boys for companions, and revel in a playground; why I don't even object to a jacket pocket! I can't say I have exactly a partiality for pockets in general, for my friends, the boys, *are* rather apt to put queer things in them, such as biscuit crumbs, beetles, fishing worms, and a host of other odds and ends, not to mention an occasional snake. But I've been very lucky, for I was a favourite alley, and have a bright red ring round me, so that I was pretty generally kept in careful quarters. Oh! how many jolly games I have had in the capital playground of Dewberry Grammar School with my owner, Ben Baily, and his chum, Bill Smith. The marbles I won for him, helped by his own good play, for he *was* a first-rate player, made quite a goodly store in his playbox. Many a boy who had been so lucky, and who played so well, would have sold them secretly to old Spattleberry, as indeed I have known some mean boys do. But Ben was an honest, open-hearted fellow, born to be a sailor, so I was not surprised to hear of him afterwards as a naval cadet, going through a course of training in the "Dreadnought" frigate. But at the time I knew him he was only a truthful, frank school-boy, very mischievous, and getting into lots of scrapes, but then they were never wicked ones, or likely to do harm to anybody, and only arising from the spirit of fun in him, that brimmed over sometimes.

I soon discovered how his hoard of marbles gradually melted away, for I saw him several times fill the empty bag of a little fellow who had lost his all, and who found a generous friend in Ben. But though he was very kind to the little ones, and liberal too in his way, nothing roused him to a regular raging passion quicker than meanness or cheating. Now little Sam Markham, who first bought me from old Spattleberry, was the meanest little sneak that ever lived, and did not care what he did, so long as he was not found out. Ben had an instinctive dislike of him, and never played with him, so that there was a sort of unspoken feud between them. Mean little Sam feared Ben's blunt, straightforward ways; and Ben had a sort of big contempt for Sam's trickfulness and shifty ways, and so they gave each other usually, what Ben would have called, a "wide berth."

But one day, Ben happened to perch himself on a very high bough of the old elm tree that stood in a corner of the playground; for he was always given to climbing, and that he knew from long experience was a secure nook to rest in away from intrusion. Many a summer holiday did he spend studying Robinson Crusoe, or Peter Simple, or something of that sort. But on this day he happened to have got "Snarley-yow," which some chum had lent him, and he was deaf and blind to almost everything. But a loud squabble under the tree at last aroused him a little, and "It's not fair, Sam; I know you're cheating," reached his ears ; and shaking himself like a waking dog, he peered down through the leaves and branches to see what was the matter. There stood Sam, his eyes twinkling, and his mouth grinning from ear to ear, as he pocketed a lot of marbles, confiscated from "blundering Bill," as William Smith was politely christened by the boys. Now Bill was a good deal younger than that little sharper, Sam, and a novice to boot in the

game, and so was not near a match for him.
Ben's honest blood boiled, and he only waited
a few minutes just to witness some most gross
cheating, and to see poor Bill turn away with
his empty bag, when he slid down the old tree
trunk like a thunderbolt, coming down upon
sly Sam, and sending all his ill-gotten gains
spinning to every corner of the playground.
Sam had the soundest thrashing he had ever
experienced, and was mulcted besides of all the
marbles he had robbed Bill of; and though
Ben was scarcely his equal in size, and a year
younger, he was far too formidable and un-
compromising an antagonist for Sam to contend
openly with. So he resigned his ill-gotten
plunder, and slunk off rubbing his shoulders,
while Ben picked up "Snarley-yow," which he
had pitched away in the beginning of the fray,
and somewhat too tired to re-climb his favourite
look-out, threw himself on a patch of grass
hard by. From that hour the friendship of
little Bill Smith and Ben was sealed and
cemented by Bill's giving and Ben's taking
me as an offering, each ignorant that I had
really originally belonged to Sam. The latter

was too cowardly to reclaim even his own, and therefore contented himself from that time by lavishing every petty but secret malignity he could devise upon the two friends. But Ben very speedily left Dewberry, and went to the Naval School, and gave me with one or two more especial favourites to Frank Spenser."

"I believe I am the next delegate," said a fine bright, speckled marble, rolling forward; "and I consider it only candid to warn you that I am not what I may appear to be. My outward looks would lead you to suppose I was made of agate, or polished stone at least, but I have really been the innocent cause of so much deception that I think it only right to state at the beginning that I am only composed of some species of chinaware, so highly glazed as to appear like a better material. We found a very ready sale at the better class of toy shops and were very popular among the young fry, who cared more for outward looks, and were not so skilful in selecting really good articles as the bigger boys.

I was purchased at the "Civet Cat," in Brompton, by little Augusta Finekyn, as a present for her brother Fred on his approaching birthday, and as I cost the large sum of four-pence, she had saved a month's pocket money for the purpose. She intended to keep me as a profound secret until the auspicious day; but her plan was really defeated by several unlucky mishaps. First of all, she dropped me in the middle of a crowded crossing, and was very nearly run over by an omnibus in her search for me, and only rescued by the old crossing sweeper. The paper in which I had been wrapped was so saturated with mud, that she was obliged to take it off and wrap me in a corner of her pocket handkerchief. When she arrived at home she took off her things, forget-ting me in her hurry, and ran down to dinner. During that meal, having occasion to want her handkerchief she drew it out of her pocket and me with it, sending me rolling among the dishes and plates, to her great dismay. However, Freddy was good-natured, and did not wish to vex his little sister, and so he pretended not to see me. Three days intervened before the birthday, and incessantly during that time did luckless Augusta contrive to drop

me about in the oddest places, putting Fred's
gravity and good humour to the sorest test
possible, and I think both were equally relieved
when the day arrived at last, and she was able
to present it in due form. Fred had plenty of
marbles of a better kind and more suitable for
playing, but he did not vex his affectionate
little sister by telling her so. For a long time
I was kept in his desk with a funny jumble of
other odds and ends not often wanted, but
never exposed to view, for poor Fred on first
returning to school had innocently exhibited
me as an *agate* marble, fully believing I really
was so. But a more knowing boy, the son of
a working jeweller who was on the same form
with him, soon undeceived him, and from that
time, with natural disgust at having been "so
green," as his schoolfellow said, Fred carefully
buried me in the recesses of his desk, and
showed me no more.

When he left school I went back among his
other valuables, and was buried for many years
in his old playbox. But one day I was rum-
maged out with a host of other antiquated
things and laid on the table. A very smart young

lady in a gay muslin dress, plentifully be-dropped with knots of ribbon, seemed to be "tidying up" as she called it; a process that appeared to me to consist in routing out and clearing away all the old hoards, and making the room as bare as an empty shop.

"Oh dear," she laughed, as I tumbled out with the rest of the boyish treasures; "here's that wretched old marble, which was *not* agate after all. The little horror! Here, Jane, give it to Cook; she wanted a marble the other day to put into her tea-kettle, and this will be just the thing for her."

And so I was consigned to Cook, and for many months continued to roll and rattle about in the bottom of her horrid old black tea-kettle, accumulating all the disagreeable "fur," as she called it, that is generally found lining the inside of a kettle where the water in use is very hard. My pretty streaks and spots soon disappeared beneath this dreadful covering, and no one now—not even Fred Finekyn himself— (far less the airyfied young lady, into whom my early admirer, Augusta, had merged), would have recognised the gay and polished marble in the rough, stony-looking lump that made such a dull clatter in the kettle.

But all things come to an end, even long captivities, and so one happy day saw me, still an inhabitant of the old kettle, sold at the sale, which took place when the Finekyns went "abroad." After this I resided for some time at a marine store-shop, and there my house and I parted company, and I was sent once more into the world as a marble, for the kettle was sold elsewhere, and I was dropped out during the examination of the old woman purchaser. When I was picked up, the shopman soon finding out that I was worth looking at, cleaned me, and restored me to a faint likeness of my former show, and sold me for the reduced price of twopence to an eager school boy. After a good many vicissitudes and changes, I came into Frank Spenser's possession, and became, with the rest, an inmate of the toy-cupboard."

The Ball, spying another little marble rolling forward as if to speak, returned thanks to them for their three stories, and called on the Rocking-Horse to be the next entertainer.

CHAPTER XI.

" COULD tell you lots of stories," said the Rocking Horse, stumbling and limping forward, as lightly as he could with his mutilated members, " for I have really seen so much of life, and have had so many little riders in turn. There was my first owner, dear bright golden-haired Charlie, "Bonnie Prince Charlie," as he was called by all, with his bright smile, and sunny eyes, and his musical laugh. He was going to be a knight-errant, and ride about all over the country, rescuing distressed damsels, and setting captives free, and fighting at least ten people at once! There was a pretty little girl, who used to come sometimes to spend the day with his sisters, and Charlie was very fond of her, calling her his princess. Little Julia was a nice child, and was never better pleased than when she was mounted on me behind Charley, with her fat arms clasped tight round his waist. The stories that boy used to invent, surpassed anything I ever heard before or since; I am sure he must have read a good deal, and remembered it all too, to be able to describe the things he did. And Julia used to cuddle up to him, and say what he bid her, for she was a sweet, docile little thing, but she did not understand a tenth part of what he told her, and she used to get so frightened, and cling so tight, and call out " O Charlie, don't rock so hard, please," when he grew excited and set me off at first rate speed. And then Charlie used to say, "You must not say that, Judy; you ought to say, Pray lessen your speed, gallant knight, your war charger is so fleet!" and Julia would say so, and all went smoothly enough till Charlie went off again full pelt, and then the whole thing was gone over again. But one day, one warm summer evening, Charlie was a little more wild than usual, and forgetting what he was about, he rocked too furiously, and down we all came together. It did not much matter to Charlie and me, for it was neither our second nor third tumble, and he used only to jump up again, and rush to see whether I was damaged, before he looked at his own bruised knees, and say, " That was a horrid spill, old boy, but never mind, we hav'nt damaged *your* knees, anyhow ! "

But this time it was a more serious case, and I lay uncared for, while Charlie scrambled hastily up, and, like a brave boy, looked first after his poor little playmate. She was more hurt than either, and lay moaning piteously, till Charlie ran in a fright and fetched his mother. When the doctor came, as he did pretty quickly, he said poor Julia's little fat arm was broken, and she could not be removed, even home. Oh, what a sad time that was; the whole household seemed to watch night and day over the little patient sufferer, and poor Charlie roamed about in a miserable and distracted way that was quite sad to see. She was delirious and in some danger for a time ; and while it lasted Charlie came and sat by me and told me all his sorrow in the most disconsolate way in the world.

" You've broken *your* leg, gallant grey," he

said to me; " but then the carpenter can mend that with no great ado, and *I've* sprained my ancle, but that's nothing, for it does not hurt much, and I can easily bear that; but I wish we had both broken all our legs, before dear little Julia had been hurt. I'm afraid I shall never be a good knight now!"

And then he laid his head on his knees, and actually cried bitterly. But all turned out better in the end, for the doctor cured Julia, and when the patient little girl grew better, all her care was to comfort Charlie, and she left her own mother (who had come to nurse her), no peace until she had formally forgiven Charlie. But poor contrite Charlie could not so readily forgive himself, and as a proof of his real wish to cure himself of his careless habits, he gave me away to Philip Reeves, an old friend of his, taking tender care to have me effectually mended up, and bidding me a most affectionate farewell. I did not like my new home very much, for though I had carried double before, little Julia was a mere feather weight, and Charlie rode very lightly; but the Reeves's children mounted me two and three at a time

played rude, practical jokes and treated me with
all sorts of indignities. Once the little wretches
actually set Tom on me with his face to my
tail, and then called me a donkey, and shouted
out, "Gee up, Neddy!" And as for falls, we
were always tumbling about,—my entire occu-
pation was tumbling about. They dragged off
all my pretty harness in tatters, by way of
hauling me up again, and then replaced it with
a horrid lot of common rope. As for my tail,
oh, that was too bad! That abominable little
Annie, the baby, got hold of me after one of
my falls, and by the help of nurse's scissors,
which had been dropped just by, she managed
to shear all the hair off close to the stump, and
disfigured me for life. Then another of my
legs was broken, past mending. And so I lost
all my good looks by degrees. To finish my
troubles, the two younger boys took it into their
heads that I wanted rubbing down, and they
set to work with a vengeance, with the help of
the nursery bath and a hard hair brush, and by
the time they were found out, the nursery was
swimming, and my poor complexion gone for
ever!

No one could stand that, and patience won't last for ever, so you cannot be surprised at my running away, and I think I managed my escape pretty luckily. One Saturday night, when the workwoman was there, her son came to fetch her home, and she somehow smuggled him into the empty nursery to wait until she was ready to go home with him. The children had all been put in their bath, and packed off early to bed, and Susan, the nursemaid, had run downstairs for a few minutes' gossip in the kitchen. Bob, the boy, began to eye me with great attention, and at last he drew near and began to play with me. His mother went to put on her bonnet and shawl, and Bob seized the opportunity.

"You be a tidy pony!" said he, "will you go along with me?"

As I made no objection, and indeed was glad to go, he whipped me up in his arms, ran down the back stairs and off with me like a shot. I was in a dreadful fright for fear we should be found out, I can tell you, for there was a wretched small woolly toy-dog, an old enemy of mine, and the little horror barked with all his might, and tried to give the alarm. But luckily for me, little Annie had that day poked a pin through the kid over his sound-hole, and so he had almost lost his voice, and was not heard at all. When I came to reflect on the matter calmly, I must own it *was* rather an undignified method of running away, but I was too anxious at the time to escape, and did not think much about it. Bob hurried down some back lanes and byeways till he reached his own door, and then he rushed in, and running upstairs, hid me under his bed. He was up in the morning long before his mother, and got me out into the back-yard, hiding me behind the old water-butt. Bob's mother happened to be that week very busy, and away every day, so that he easily kept me out of the way. There was a nice hue and cry at the Reeves's when the children found out I had vanished, and Bob's mother came home each day, giving him a full history of the loss, little suspecting he was concerned in it.

But evil deeds seldom meet with thorough success, and so Bob found out, for a playfellow of his, it seems, had watched enough of his pro-

ceedings to find out that all was not right, and
one day he attacked him on the subject. Bob
was in a terrible fright, and at last made up his
mind to take me back to the Reeves's again,
hoping to smuggle me in after the same fashion
he had brought me away. I was not much improved, as you may fancy, after being stabled
so long behind that dirty tarred barrel. Indeed,
I think the Reeves's children might almost have
met me without recognising me. But they
were not destined to be put to the trial, for just
as Bob got near to the door, out sallied a whole
tribe of the young ones, bound for a late walk.
Bob beat a precipitate retreat, and pitched me
headlong into a big laurel hedge, near the gate.
As it proved afterwards, the children had not
seen me, and so there I lay all night, when a
drenching rain came down, and washed off all
the paint I had left. I was now a poor wreck
of a thing, and did not look as if I was of any
value, and I was so out of heart and miserable,
that I did not care what became of me. So
when I was picked out of the hedge by Bill
Soames, and carried to his cottage-home as a
precious treasure, I was resigned to my fate.

Horses, said I to myself, are peculiarly liable to these ups and downs of life, for, as we all know, the spirited racer that wins the Challenge Cup, may end his days harnessed to a cart. And so why should I lament my fate! I dare say, Bill Soames will be kind to me, and he looks as if he could ride. And so he could too, and many a prance we had on the brick floor of that old cottage, for in spite of my lame legs and docked tail, there was a little life and spirit left still in the poor old nag. And through all my life, I have been *very* lucky in one thing, my foundations were good! Let what would happen to my legs or tail, at any rate, my rockers never came off! So I could get on pretty fairly even now, and Bill was as proud of me as if I had been a real flesh and blood steed.

Many and many a box on the ears did he get from his mother, for picking her lilac or her roses to stick in my ears; and the day when she gave him some old scraps of dirty ribbon was a joyous day for him. The only pity was that his wish to adorn me to the best advantage led him in a weak moment to accept the proposal of George Hall, the little painter,

who offered to make me as good as new! I
can't bear to think of it, much less describe
that operation, and you may take my word for
it I should have run away again, if I had not
been tied up to the leg of the great wooden
table. Bill remarked that he had seen the
farrier singe and clip horses, and he always
took good care to tie them up tight first. And
so there I was at their mercy, and I came out
of their hands such a figure, that I only wonder
the nervous old cat, who lived there too, did
not have a fit at the first sight of me. I had
been painted black, with great white spots, just
like big white wafers plentifully besprinkled all
over me; and they had picked out my eyes and
nose with such bright red borders, that it
looked as if I breathed fire and flame, and I
should have made a capital steed for the
Fire-King in the pantomine. Bill was so
delighted with me, that when I was dry and fit
to be touched, he took more pains and care of
me than ever. He stabled me in a corner,
always offered me a share of his supper (but,
as you may suppose, I don't eat bread and
cheese), and covered me over from the dust
with the counterpane of his own bed.

So I was obliged to make the best of it, and bear my terrible disfigurement as well as I could, for the sake of the good, warm-hearted lad, who loved me so very dearly. And at last I got used to my new colour, and even the atrocious spots, for everybody round was always admiring me, and praising my beauty; and I began to think I was not so very bad after all, till one day, when the memory of all my reverses and troubles seemed to come back over me like a thunderbolt. I was standing out on the little green space before the cottage, in the sun, as I often did, for Bill was very fond of mounting and riding in the sight of all passers by. There was a low green quickset hedge dividing the cottage garden from the road, and a open wooden gate. I heard a voice say, "I'll be shot if that ain't the very likeness of him. If he were only of a dirty white, and hadn't no spots, I'd say for certain it were he. There's a lump in his hind leg looks uncommon like the jine where he were broken!"

Just at this moment, George Hall and Bill came out of the cottage door, and the speaker shuffled off rather fast, but not until I had managed to catch a glimpse of him, and had recognised my old friend Bob, with whom I had first eloped. And the very next day, when I was out as usual, who should come by but "Bonnie Prince Charlie," hand in hand with little Julia. I declare the few hairs of my mane and tail fairly stiffened at the sight of them, and I longed to be able to trot out like a fairy horse and ask them to get on my back, and let me carry them off to some delightful island, and make them a real prince and princess! Dear little Julia, she had not quite got back her nice rosy fat cheeks, but her eyes were as bright, and her merry voice as sweet as ever, as she prattled merrily to Charlie, who watched over her in the most careful way, guarding the poor lame arm quite jealously from harm. I heard them before I saw them, and knew their dear voices, bless them! in a moment.

"You shall have a carriage and pair, Judy, at least," said Charlie, "and a gentle mare for riding on, with a long tail and flowing mane. And you will be able to plait them up with ribbons, as Camilla did, you know, for Black Auster."

"I would rather have a little Shetland pony," said Julia, "I'm *so* afraid of big horses, Charlie!"

"Why a pony is the most dangerous of all, Julia," replied Charley with a learned air; "it is so much more frisky, and apt to run away. But we'll take care to have one that's warranted to carry a lady."

"But I'm not a real grown-up lady yet, am I?" said the innocent little girl, turning her blue wondering eyes full on Charlie, who she evidently thought the most wonderful hero in the world. Charlie laughed, and pulled her curls, and said he hoped he should be able to take better care of her when *he* was bigger, "better than I *have* done, Ju," he added, somewhat dolefully; "I shall not forget that spill with Gallant Grey in a hurry. What a jolly horse he was too, and how delighted I was when Papa let me choose him at that lovely shop in London, where they sell nothing but horses, and a little girl sits and rocks on one in the window, you know. Poor old Gallant Grey, I wonder how he's getting on, and whether Phil Reeves has had as many spills as I have.

But halloa, Ju, here's a queer thing! why, if there is not a rocking-horse in that little garden!"

As Bonnie Prince Charlie and his little princess stood hand-in-hand at the gate and peeped at me with surprise through the rails, I could have eaten my head with vexation to think I could not even neigh a "how d'ye do?" to them.

"My eyes," said Charlie, as he slowly turned away, "what an old nag *that* is! not a bad made animal, but what a colour, and what spots! What can he be? Perhaps they're going to have Guy Faux on horseback, and are getting ready the steed!"

And off went Charlie and Julia, and I could hear their merry voices ringing with laughter, for a long way down the lane. If it had only been in my nature to cry, I should have shed red hot tears of vexation, enough to burn up the little grass plat I stood on. I never saw Charlie and Julia again, and lived for a long while a sort of humdrum existence with Bill Soames. But life seemed very flat after that sad mortification, and I never went on the little grass plat again without remembering it. And

time passed on, and when Bill grew bigger and
went out to work, he gave me away to another
chum, who was a horrid sailor boy, and had no
more notion of riding than a teaspoon. He
soon grew tired of me, and passed me on to some
one else.   And so have I served many masters,
and have in my time been kept in some very
queer stables. But I never cared for any of
my subsequent owners so much as I did for
Charlie, and Bill Soames, for they were all
dull, uninteresting boys, who treated me as a
mere toy, and cared less for me than a top or a
kite.

When I came to Harry Spenser, however, I
began to think I was going to have a sort of
second life, and be happy once more. The
first thing that made me take to him was that
he saved up his pocket money till he could
afford to have me re-painted. I was now a
bright bay, with a white star on my forehead,
and though I bore a good many marks of ill
usage and former accidents, and both my knees
were broken, still at a distance I looked pretty
well.   Harry's little brother, Frank, thought me
perfection, and christened me " Bay Middleton,"

and had many a pleasant ride on me. But
Harry was just in all the delight of the perusal
of the Arabian nights, and could think of
nothing but the Enchanted Horse, and he
played at being Prince Firouz Schah, till I was
quite tired of it. He drove two huge nails in
my neck to serve for the two pegs that he was
to turn, the one to raise him up among the
clouds like a bird, and the other to lower him
to earth once more. The latter peg is still
here, as you may see, behind my ear, but they
never performed that feat with me, for Harry was
not magician enough to endow me with flying
powers. He tried very hard to get Celia to
play the part of the Princess of Bengal, but
though she was very willing and obliging, and
tried to do what he wished, she was too big to
ride behind him, and he did not think her quite
majestic enough for the part. At last, when
Harry went off to Eton, I was put away here,
and though for a time I indulged in a faint
hope that he might look for me on his return
for the holidays, I was disappointed, and even
Frank has never looked for me since. And so
now, my friends, I have given you a history of

all that has befallen me, including the famous episode of my running away."

The Toys, who had been much amused by the relation of the Rocking Horse, more particularly by the grave manner in which he spoke, to which his very rackety and dilapidated appearance lent a ludicrous effort, now thanked him very heartily for his story, and proceeded to call on the Skipping-rope for the next story.

CHAPTER XII.

THE MISHAP OF THE SKIPPING-ROPE.

"STORY," said the Skipping-rope, "to be sure you shall have it, and a very queer one. it is, quite the oddest of the lot, I rather think. But I shall be very happy to begin it at once, if the Kite will be so good as to disentangle his tail."

"Pshaw," growled the Kite, "why, I was obliged to tell mine while you were tugging at me all the while. Two or three times, when I had something very particular to say, you pulled my tail suddenly, and I lost the thread of my discourse. So tit for tat, my friend, do you unwind ur yarn, and I won't serve you any worse than you d' me."

The Skipping-rope, finding she could not gain her point, gave herself a spiteful wriggle, which nearly tore off the grand tassel at the end of the Kite's tail, and set off full gallop in her recital, leaving him no breathing time to complain :—

"I began life," said she, "as a mere length of rope, although I only form now a small portion of the coil to which I belonged. I was the property of a poor fisherman, who lived in a hut belonging to a cluster of storm-beaten cots, called by great courtesy, the 'village' of Rocksand, in Devonshire. All the people who lived there were very poor, and gained a precarious living by fishing, while their wives occupied the spare time left after "keeping house, and minding the childer," by cultivating the very small bits of garden ground that belonging to them, and which were situated on the top of a very lofty cliff, some height above the nestling cottages which were huddled under its shelter on the shore, not so very far above the high tide line. Indeed, in stormy weather, the rough seas which churned the restless pebbles on the beach, se : their waves in very adverse weather, and during winds that set dead in shore, into somewhat disagreeable nearness to the doorsteps! And as for the spray, well! in storms it put out the fires, by falling down the low wide chimneys, but in ordinary weather people never minded it.

As for the children, they were like little ducklings, and directly they were big they took to the water like young Newfoundland puppies; and while they were too small for that, they played in it, and made " sand pies," for there was no mud there, and became dirty and draggled, and therefore happy to their heart's content. And a rare hardy, ruddy set they were, living on the very scantiest and coarsest fare, and thriving on the salt fresh breezes, like young giants, as they were. My owner was a tall, strong young man, who supported his wife and two little ones by his own incessant hard work. He was a capital climber too, and was very fond of scrambling about the face of the cliff in almost inaccessible places for birds' nests and eggs, of which he had quite a large collection. He used to blow and preserve the eggs, replace them in their pretty and curious nests, and then offer them for sale in the neighbouring town. He also collected the samphire growing on the rocky masses that jutted out into the sea, and for which his wife found a

ready sale in the town market. They were
frugal, hard-working people, but they often
found it very difficult to provide food and
clothing for their little ones, and to keep the
boat and nets in good repair. I am proud to
say I was a very useful member of the family,
and was wanted everywhere. During the intervals of time, when my services were not required
in the boat, I did duty as a clothes line, which
rather grated against my dignity, for I fancied
it was not the sort of work I ought to be set to
do. However, I consoled myself with the re-
flection that I had nothing to do with common
clothes props or garden walls, for I was generally stretched out on the beach, in a sheltered
nook behind the cottage. One end was tied
fast to an old mast that now bore a weathercock,
and the other was fastened to a ring in a piece
of rock, near by. So I was patiently contented
to hold up all the family wardrobe to dry, for it
was not a very large one, and I knew every-
time exactly what I should have to carry. And
the sea winds were very obliging, and dried all
the clothes so fast, that my patience was not
much tested.

I tethered the little boat to her landing-place close by, and many a time has Mary been only too glad to lay hold of me, when her husband threw me ashore, after a long night's buffeting with the winds and waves. Even little Robin came behind her and gave fierce tugs at me, to " draw daddie home again!" Once I saved his father's life, so precious to all that little family, for he would have been sorely missed, while there were so many young mouths to feed. It so happened on the day I mean, that he had taken me out with him, not a usual thing unless it threatened stormy weather. But that morning, when he set out early, the sky was as blue and cloudless as on a bright summer's day, and there was hardly a puff of wind going. He put up his little sail, but it flapped almost lazily against the mast, and he and his " mate," as he called the old boatman (who was a sort of second partner in the boat and fishing gear), had to take to their oars and row to the fishing stakes and nets. They had taken a good stock of fish, and were thinking of getting back with the tide, when a sudden squall arose, beginning with " the little black cloud, as big as a man's

hand," and ending in a fierce wind, that soon
lashed the sea up into big mountains of waves.
The fisherman, while prudently watching and
carefully managing his sail, had stood on the
seat of the boat, but a sudden gust coming as the
wind chopped round to another point, he stepped
hastily on the side, his foot slipped on the wet
edge, and he overbalanced and fell into the
raging waves. The old boatman, who was
used to mishaps at sea, dropped the tiller, and
rushed to his mate's assistance, and when he
came to the surface threw an end of my rope to
him. By the help of this and the oar, he managed with some difficulty, and after he had
swam some time alongside, by my help to drag
him on board again, though with no small danger of upsetting the frail skiff. They were some
time in getting back, for the poor fellow was
rather exhausted by his ducking and long swim
in the water, and could not pull the oar with his
usual skill. After that feat, I was still more
valued, and invariably taken out in the boat in
case of future accidents.

And now the summer came on, and with it
the busiest time of the women of Rocksand,

for most of them were hard at work early and late in their little patches of garden ground. The fishermen generally left all these matters to their wives, but my master was an industrious young man, and was not particular what he turned his hand to, so that he might often have been seen in the potato ground, hoeing and weeding, while his mates were lying on the shore watching the weather or smoking their pipes at the cottage doors. Just now, the crop of potatoes was being dug, and so John Pike and his wife were hard at work on their ridges. It was a long trudge from the village, and the weather was hot, so Mary had brought both her children with her. The youngest, about two years old, she had laid on an old shawl under the hedge, and there he sat propped up, and mighty busy over a basket of shells she had brought up for him to play with. The elder boy, about five, was trotting about very soberly, so that they did not watch him perhaps as keenly as they ought, and so he scrambled through a hole in the fence to the next field, and somehow managed to tumble into the old well there. The fright of his parents on hearing his shrieks may be imagined but not described, and they both rushed to the direction the sound came from. John soon saw what was the matter, and running back, snatched me hastily up, and ran to the side of the well. It was luckily an old one, long unused, and in consequence of the dry weather had but little water. It took John very few seconds to throw one end of me hastily but tightly round a tree close by, and let himself down. He got hold of the little fellow, and climbed out again with my help, laying him on the grass, when he got him out. For a long time they thought the child was dead; but they carried him home, and very luckily met the village doctor on their way, by whose skill, after long, long persevering efforts he was brought slowly to life. But for many a month after that he was ill from the combined effects of the shock, the bad air, the fright, and the water. Indeed, as the doctor said, he must have spent a cat's nine lives in getting through it at all.

It was a sad trial for poor John and his wife, although they bore it patiently enough, only thankful that their Robin was spared to them.

But his mother had no time to give to her crops now, and John had more than he could manage with his fishing besides, and was not able to make it as profitable as usual. But all their poor neighbours were very kind to them, and would always bring in any bit of more tempting food than they usually had, for poor little Robin. He lay patient enough on his hard bed, and was very cheerful and bright when his illness would allow it. His father had delighted him beyond measure by tying me to the top of his bed, so that he could drag himself up into a sitting posture by my help, and he fancied himself quite a sailor, and used to lie there smiling, and talking in a low voice to himself about the ropes and rigging of a ship. Old Bill, the boatman, his father's mate, had made him a little boat, and while he was finishing it, he used to sit by poor Robin's bedside, and tell him all about the different parts of a ship, so that the child (who was naturally quick, and was now no doubt made more so by his illness, and long rest), soon became quite knowing about the different sails and ropes.

"This is a sloop, Bill, aint it," he used to

say, "'cause she's only got one mast. I should like to have a brig with two masts, and lots of sails!"

Poor little Robin! he was never well again, for, as it seemed afterwards, his spine had received some injury from the fall, which it never recovered. He only lived to be twelve years old, and during that time could never get about like other boys, and was continually laid up, especially in the cold winter season, for months together. But as his body became so weak, his mind seemed to grow instead, and he was more like a man than a child in his thoughts and ways, though *always* patient. He improved on his old tutor's lessons too, and became quite a skilful boat maker, and turned out some very pretty little wooden models of ships and boats, all properly rigged, which his mother sold for him in the market at the town hard by. He was able by these means to add a little to the family fund, and though his gains were, of course, but small, it was better than being a helpless burthen upon his poor parents, and the light work whiled away many a weary hour of suffering and pain for him. Through all the years that had passed since his accident, I had been left still tied to the tester of his bed, and I still served to help him to drag up his feeble limbs, and to turn in bed, for he was very feeble, poor fellow.

But I was destined to play an important part once more, and for the last time in the family history. When Robin was about twelve years old, there came a very severe winter, which was sorely felt all through the little fishing village, and by none more heavily than the poor fisherman's family. The fishing turned out badly, and the previous potato crop having been a scanty one, they barely found enough to live upon. Poor Robin had been more than usually delicate and ailing during that winter, and suffered more than the rest from all the privations. The spring drew on drearily enough, cold, dull, and cheerless, so that there scarcely seemed a glimpse of hope of better days. One day when John was almost out of heart and hope, he set off on a long ramble, hoping by diligent climbing and search to find at any rate a few rare birds' nests in the crevices of the cliffs. Everything had gone worse even than usual, there had been no fish caught worth mentioning for many days, and John's poor old patched and mended nets were rapidly falling to pieces in spite of all his care, while he was not able to buy enough bread for the little household, not to mention material for new nets. So he climbed wearily on, and rounded rock after rock, meeting with but little success, till at last he had reached a long distance from home, and had climbed a good way up one of the tallest cliffs in the neighbourhood. He was rewarded by finding a couple of rare nests full of eggs, and with renewed hope he climbed eagerly on. He saw one just a little above him, but in a very awkward place to get at, for there was a cleft in the rock he must leap over to get at it. He had a steady head and a light foot, and took the leap without hesitation, when, to his horror, as he alighted on the other side a piece of the mouldering stone broke off, and fell rolling down with a loud noise, crumbling to pieces as it bounded down the sharp rocky face of the cliff. There was now too wide a space between for him to risk the return, and there he stood on a narrow ledge of rock, with the sharp peaks

and the roaring sea beneath him, and a steep
wall of cliff stretching up above his head.
John Pike was a brave man, and had been used
to face many a danger, but the blood seemed
to leave his heart, and his breath almost stopped,
as he understood the full peril of his position.
It was indeed a serious one, and as he thought
over the scant chance there was of any help or
rescue, he covered his face with his hands and
groaned in agony for those at home, more than
for himself. And while he stood there, despair-
ing of all human aid, many a prayer went up
from his heart's core to God for help for the
sake of his wife and poor Robin. And then he
set to work with all his best energy to make his
terrible position known. He had fortunately a
handkerchief in his pocket, and this he tied to
the walking-stick he always took with him on his
climbing expeditions. He shouted at frequent
intervals in the hope of making some one hear,
and at last, to his great joy, he espied a little
figure below on the distant beach! It was
a poor shrimper, with her nets on her back,
returning home, and she saw at a glance how
the case stood, and hastened at once to the

JACK IN JEOPARDY.

Page 188.

village to give an alarm. In a shorter space of time than could have been hoped even, John saw a number of his fellow fishermen hastening down the beach to him. He could not catch their words, but he understood from their signs that they found it would be impossible to get him down again, and so they were going to mount the cliff, and try and get at him that way. As they passed the village on their way to the top of the cliff, poor Mary rushed out wildly to them, for she had by accident heard the truth, anxiously as her kind neighbours had tried to prevent it. They hastily told her their plans, and asked her for the longest ropes she had, as they would want all they could get. She hurriedly dragged me down, and rushed after them, for, as she said, she could not stay at home, while her husband was in such peril, and she must see the worst with her own eyes. When they reached the top of the cliff, the fishermen hastily rigged up a sort of rude windlass, and knotting the lengths of rope firmly together, they succeeded in making a line long enough to reach him, and firm enough to bear him. It was an anxious time, while they gradually drew him up the steep face of the cliff. They did not dare to pull quickly, for fear he should be dashed against the rock and lose his hold, and they were also afraid of grazing the rope against the jagged rocks. But at last, with great care, and by his own prudent management and skill in guiding the rope, he was landed safely on the top of the cliff. Poor Mary was so overjoyed at his escape, that when they all turned to go home, and were tying up the rope again, she caught me up, and declared she should value me to her dying day. Strangely enough, I was the only rope that was damaged of all, for I had been chafed a good deal against the rock, and in one place was nearly cut through. For a long while after Mary shuddered so at the sight of that piece of me, that at last Robin, who had regained possession of me, cut me through. The longer piece was kept for the boat, and the shorter length you now behold was tied up again for poor Robin's use as before.

There was not one in the village who did not heartily rejoice at John's rescue; and it almost seemed as if after that things had come to the worst, for they began to mend. There were more fish taken than had been known on that coast for many years, and the weather proved most fortunate for getting in the humble crops, so that John had some new nets at last; and the poor family had enough to eat. But better food and brighter days could not save poor Robin; the long winter had told too heavily upon him to enable him to rally again. By the time the blackberries were in flower on the top of the cliff, Robin had faded away, like their leaves, but very patient, very happy to the last. His mother had fancied him asleep, as he lay so quietly with one of my ends still held fast in his wasted fingers. His mother fretted so for him, and took his loss so sadly to heart, that it was pitiable to see her. The sight of his vacant bed, and the cord still hanging there, seemed to go like a knife to her heart; and therefore John took me away one day without her knowledge, and put me out of sight.

I was forgotten for many years, so many indeed, that when I next came to daylight I found everything strange and altered in the cottage. John and his wife, grown old and past work, had gone to live in another house, better sheltered from the wind, and one of their children, now married, had settled there instead. I was tossed about for a long while, for no one now living knew my real history, and had therefore little value for me, and indeed I was more especially held in dislike by the young ones, as affording them just that taste of "the rope's end" that they did not covet.

The end of my career was that of being tied round a box, when one of the daughters went to service, and left Rocksand, and thus I came to town. My life here had nothing remarkable in it; I was put to my present use one day when one of the young Spensers was taken with a passion for skipping. They declared I was heavier and better than all the smart skipping-ropes to be bought at the toy shop, and made such continual use of me, that I am really almost threadbare. But I was poked away in this cupboard on the occasion of some great nursery clearing, and here I have lived ever since."

"How you must have regretted your freedom," said the Kite, in a sympathising tone;

"I feel myself sometimes quite what I may call sky-sick! I would give all my tassels and fringes for one more good flight through the clear air. When I think of the bright sun, and the nice fleecy clouds, I am almost inclined to tumble to pieces for grief, to think I can't get out of this horrid, dusty stuffy hole of a toy cupboard, as they call it! A prison *I* consider it, and a cruel one too!"

"I *would* give anything I could," sighed the old Skipping-rope, "for even one breath of the fresh salt sea breeze. I think of the dancing waves glittering in the sun, till I feel quite giddy. But it is no use repining, and after all, really this little break on the monotony of our existence is very pleasant."

"It *is* very pleasant," assented the Ball, "but I am afraid our time to-night at any rate grows very short, for it is almost dark, and that terrible old woman will be coming back. So with your leave, my friends, I will call upon the Humming Top for his story."

CHAPTER XIII.

THE HUMMING TOP'S HISTORY.

HE Humming Top, who had begun to fear he should not be allowed a chance of speaking at all, and who felt just a little put out at coming so late in the list, gave himself a majestic twirl, and spun for a minute or two before he condescended to speak. At last, when he had reached a commanding position, he leaned gracefully back, and commenced his story in a very grand manner and air :—

"As I perceive, my friends, that your curiosity is more directed to our adventures in the world, than to our origin and construction, and as few of you have discoursed upon your native places and earliest histories, I will not trouble you with mine. Sufficient to the purpose is it that I made my first appearance in the world on a large stall in the Soho Bazaar, which was then in all its early glory. I was then, I may say, splendid in appearance, for I was painted in many brilliant hues, and there was no lack of gilding about me, so that when I was properly spun, I appeared like a gorgeous flower, all one mass of dazzling hues. Indeed, when the lady who superintended the stall took me out of the folds of silver paper in which I was carefully wrapped, she laughed, and said to her assistant, 'why surely this must be the King of the Humming Tops!' I was placed in a very prominent position among all the gay toys which adorned the counter, and I must say they were all exceedingly nice in their behaviour, and paid a great deal of respect to me. Many pleasant days I passed there with my companions, for I was of a rather high price, and those were dear times for articles of luxury and pleasure. We had no cheap twopenny and penny toys then, for it was long before Christmas trees became generally known in England. I have always regretted the inroads of those new comers, because they have introduced so many cheap toys—penny toys, indeed; fancy a whole stall devoted to penny toys!"

"I must beg entirely to disagree with you," interrupted the Ball; "I for one most distinctly say, that I don't see why all these simple pleasures should be kept for rich children only. I am sure our friend, the Teapot, in the course of her story, gave us a very truthful description of the value of toys to the poor children."

"If I may be allowed to speak again," said the Teapot, eagerly, "I would say with all my strength that I am glad of the cheapness of common toys. I am sure the Humming Top has never seen what I have; how should he, mixing up, as he has done, with only the better class of playthings? But if I were asked," continued the little motherly Teapot, getting quite warm on the subject—"if I were asked 'What was the good of toys?' I should reply, 'To please poor children.'"

"I quite agree with you," remarked the Toy Kitchen; "and though, as I said before, I am not very clever at explaining my meaning, I should like to say a few words too. I have spent most of my life among the poor, as I have told you before, and I have often thought that whoever invented toys must have meant them first of all for the poor, more particularly the poor little children who live in great cities. Now, there is an old proverb, I often heard my old master repeat, that 'All work and no play makes Jack a dull boy,' and he said it was the truest word ever spoken. And if the better-off children want a little play to liven up their days, when they are fed with plenty of good food, and live in pure air, their hardest work being book lessons, what must poor children do, who very often earn their very scanty living from the cradle almost? Our good friend, the Teapot, has told us how the sight of a halfpenny toy will bring such delight to little dim eyes, and skinny faces, as must be pleasant to see; so I for one say with all my might, 'Prosperity, and plenty of it, to the cheap toys!'"

The Humming Top was quite disgusted with this long discussion, and pooh-poohed it all as very low; but the number of votes was against him, so with an offended roll round, he took up the thread of his story.

"Well, there is no accounting for tastes, and so I will say no more, only that I have been brought up so entirely among people of the better classes, that I cannot say much on any other subject. I told you before that I lay for some time unsold, on account of the highness of my price, and during that time made acquaintance with many sets of companions,—dolls, boxes of soldiers, and various others. At last, to my great joy, I was selected by a lady for her little daughter, and taken home to a very nice large house in Russell Square.

Little Mary was an only child, and was therefore the idol of her parents; but, although she was much indulged, she was not by any means a spoiled child. Used as she had been from her cradle to the companionship of much older persons, she was a quiet, well-behaved little damsel enough. Her father and mother were not at all young, and having neither brothers nor sisters to play with, Mary naturally knew and felt little of the riotous gaiety of a child. The nursery was as tidy and as neatly arranged as any room in that handsome but formal house, and the *litter* of playthings was not much known there in those days. Mary had one or two dolls, very smartly dressed, but the prim little damsel played with them in a sort of grave, old-fashioned, motherly way that had no childishness in it. Her books were kept on a small book-shelf hung up on purpose, and her toys were put away in orderly fashion in a drawer.

How happy I was! for I was used carefully and well, never flung violently about or used roughly, and my little mistress had a dainty way of spinning me that would have won the affection of the hardest and sternest of Humming Tops. During all the years I lived with her, I never saw her look untidy, or with a spot or soil on frock or pinafore, nor did I ever know her to be anything but placid and gentle, very happy but very grave. So it was no wonder her father and mother loved her so dearly, and lavished on her every comfort and pleasure that money could purchase. And she grew up to be a very sweet, quiet girl, the comfort of her old parents, and beloved more in her own home than anywhere else. She did not care for gaiety much, nor wish to go to many parties or plays, and even when she did, she was so modest and retiring in her manner that she was often passed over without much notice, and very few would have known her for the rich heiress that she was. And this of course, you know, was long after we had parted company. For, strange to say, she seemed to grow younger in some things, as she grew older in years, and when she was fifteen or sixteen, she looked more of a child than she did when she was really little. She had a simple, earnest way with her that was very pleasant, and she was fond of her old toys till she grew up. I don't mean to say she played with us then, but she valued us as the treasures of her childhood, her happy childhood, and put us carefully away as old friends. Indeed, as far as I am concerned, I may even date our intimate fellowship far later than this, for when she was a woman grown, she would often take me out in a sort of musing way, and say, 'Come, old Busy Bee, and give me a little of your humming?' She called me 'old Busy Bee,' you must know, as a sort of pet nickname. And you may be sure I put on my best waltzing powers, and hummed like twenty Dumbledores in a churn! And as she grew up she had plenty of suitors, and her parents wished her to go out sometimes to grand balls and parties, so that she was much admired and followed. I have often known her come home from one of these, and come into her room, and, throwing off her rich dress and ornaments, she would sit down by a little table and take me out and spin me in a sort of absent way.

"Busy Bee, there are plenty come wooing to little plain, quiet Mary; what shall she say, Busy Bee? Come, hum me an answer!"

And then I hummed away loudly, and told her that she was so good and sweet, that she was fit for any lord in the land. But she would always wilfully misunderstand me, and she would reply:—

"You are right, Busy Bee! I must never leave the dear father and mother; if the king himself came a wooing, I would make him a low curtsey, Busy Bee, like this, and say, 'No, I thank your Majesty!'"

"But at last a day came when the kind, loving old father was taken ill, and carried to his long home, and his faithful old wife did not very long survive him, and so poor Mary was left all alone. I say poor Mary, for though she had plenty of money, and houses, and dresses, and fine jewels, not to speak of hosts of busybody relations who were always looking her up, she had lost the tender love that had been her joy from infancy. And hers was one of those loving natures that are shaken to the very core of their hearts by these heavy sorrows, which break up all the firm foundations of a young life, and that however bravely they may be borne, as they were indeed in her case, poor dear, are long felt, and suffered. Our merry evening gossips had ceased for a long time, and indeed I had almost begun to fancy I was intended to be the inhabitant of the drawer for the rest of my life. An old Fan who had slipped in with us by accident, told me that Mary had been abroad for many months with an aunt of hers, and that she might not return for some time. One night, however, I heard an unusual bustle in the neighbourhood, and presently our drawer was pulled open by a hand whose touch thrilled me in a moment, for I knew it was that of my dear mistress.

" Poor old Busy Bee," said she, softly, " you and I have not hummed together for a long while, so come out of your hiding place, old friend, and hum away as pleasantly as you used to do!"

As you may suppose, I was not slow to obey the summons, and I was soon spinning and humming on the table before her, and telling her in my way how very glad I was to see her once more. But she did not listen to me this night, and even let me roll off the table more than once, holding me in one hand after she picked me up, and absently threading me without the key.

"Well, Busy Bee," she said at last, softly, "we are going a long, long journey, and I daresay shall not see the old house again for many, many years! I wonder if you will hum as well in India, Busy Bee, or whether the hot, sultry air there will cause you to be drowsy. But it does not matter whether it is hot or cold, so long as you are happy! Go back to night to your place in the drawer, and to-morrow you shall be packed carefully away in one of those grand new trunks Morris is so proud of and so busy over. You will have a trip on the deep, deep sea, and when you next come out you will perhaps see palm trees and black people! You will have to learn Hindostanee, Busy Bee, and forget all your English ways of humming."

Then my mistress put me carefully back in the drawer, and I lost no time in telling the fan what delightful things were in store for us, and we both dropped asleep planning what we should do in India, though not before we had had a vehement quarrel, for the Fan gave herself such airs, and said we were going out entirely on her account, for that she had many relations in that country, and the heads of the family were called Punkahs, and were high in office there. But we were both doomed to disappointment, for time passed on, and we never came out of our drawer after all. We did not know any more until a long, long while afterwards, when we were routed out of the drawer by accident, by the old housekeeper. "Bless my heart, Ann," said she, "dear Miss Mary, or, as I should say, Mrs. Warren, never took her poor little old treasures after all. I suppose Morris forgot to look in this drawer, for I know she cleared all the rest. I'll be bound how sorry she was when she unpacked at Calcutta, and

missed them. If we get a chance, Maynard, we'll
send these over to her, when another box goes."

This was a terrible blow to us, to find that
our dear young mistress had married and gone
away to India without us. The fan was incon-
solable, and led me such a life with her groans
and sighs that I wished myself anywhere else,
and could only hope old Mrs. Jones would be
as good as her word and send us over. But
she never did, and there we lay no doubt for
many years almost untouched. From what I
could find out from stray bits of news, the house
was left in the charge of the old Aunt with whom
Mary had lived after the death of her parents,
and who now had two daughters living with
her, both middle-aged women, and one of them
a widow. So there were no young children in
the house, and we never heard merry voices nor
pattering feet, nor saw any little faces in the
deserted room. I was always of a more quiet
nature, and so I bore my long captivity better
than the Fan did. She, poor frivolous, fluttering
thing, could only lament over the balls and
parties she had once known, and sigh over her
imprisonment.

But the longest day must come to an end at last, and so ours did, for we were aroused from our lethargy by a little shrill voice, which cried, "O Mamma, which is the drawer where the toys were kept?"

"Here, my darling," answered a soft, low voice, which vibrated through every fibre of both the fan and myself, for we recognised the tones of our dear mistress once more. And then we saw her too, for the long-closed drawer was opened at last, and we beheld her, a slender, sweet-looking woman, with her little daughter, Ellen, by her side. We could have fancied from her size that our own little Mary was there again, but when she looked round, her sallow complexion, bright, restless eyes, and long dark hair, plainly bespoke the little Indian-born child.

"May I have all these for my very own, dear Mamma?" asked she, in her little eager voice.

"Yes, Nelly, you may if you like, on condition you take care of my poor old playthings, especially this Humming Top, which I used to call my Busy Bee, Nelly, when I was young. It was given to me when I was a little child;

but then *I* was very careful of *my* toys, and put them away neatly when I had done with them, very unlike a little girl I know, but we won't mention names, who destroys her toys sadly."

But Nelly was too busy over her fresh hoard to listen to any warnings, and for a little while she kept her word, and put us away when she had done playing with us. But this did not last long, for she was a careless child, *very* different to her dear mother. I had been secretly hoping that my good mistress would take me under her especial charge again, and that I should see a little more of her. But I suppose she was too busied with her many cares and occupations now, and she had so long broken off all her old habits and ways of thinking, that she hardly seemed like the same. But you see she had been away all these years, and perhaps passed through many changes, and had lost these old memories to which we clung so fast.

As for Nelly, Oh! what a child she was, as different to her mother as night to day; noisy and active, restless and wild spirited, the old house echoed as, it had not done for many generations. There was more untidiness, uproar, and trouble in one week now than had been seen in three years before. As for the poor old nursery, how Mrs. Warren could come in as calmly, and smile as she did, seeming pleased at all the disorder and her little girl's high spirits—*rudeness*, *we* called it—we could never understand. The poor Fan used to wave mournfully at me sometimes with the few sticks she had left, and really I almost believe we half regretted our old quiet. Miss Nelly was more fond of the Fan than anything, and gave it plenty of employment, almost wearing it out in doing so; but she turned up her little pert nose at me, and called me a prosy old drone! Yes, actually, you may well be surprised, but after I had been spinning with all my might, and humming the best air I knew, she would push me roughly from her, and go off to something else. To be sure it was her way with everything, for she brought home a number of pretty Indian toys, all made of wood, and painted in very gay colours with beautiful varnish; but these she utterly despised and flung about. They would have been quite tip-top society at a bazaar or in a fancy fair, and the poor things felt their degradation keenly, only being foreigners, they could not make themselves so easily understood. But I could repeat such tales to you that they told me of their native country, and their makers!"

CHAPTER XIV.

JUST at this moment the Humming Top was suddenly interrupted by a violent, loud noise which checked his humming pretty quickly, and startled all the rest of the toys so much, that they rolled and rattled back into their shelter, the toy cupboard, as speedily as they could.

"Vich of the painters is a coming to-morrow, Seusan, my child," said old Mrs. Jones, the charwoman, as she popped her head in at the door, and held up a tall dip in a tin candlestick to see if all was safe.

"Well, I thought I'd a shet up these here windows," said she, "but I s'pose I didn't, and the wind must have blowed the cupboard door open, and sent these here old playthings all over the room. Come in, my dear, and just help me to put them in again, will ye?"

And with Susan's help, old Mrs. Jones made a complete, clean sweep of all the poor dilapidated toys, huddled them roughly back into their cupboard, and shut the door, not only turning the button firmly, but locking it as well.

"Them painter chaps," said Mrs. Jones, as she put the key in her great dimity pocket, "is'nt to be trusted no ways. They're as likely to shy all them old playthings out o' winder as not, and then the poor children would miss 'em when they come home."

And so the room was once more left to stillness and darkness for the night. The little mice came out and ran riot about the bare floor, and tried to get into the cupboard, but they could not manage it; and the crickets chirped loudly in the distant kitchen, for they were so used to Mrs. Jones, they did not mind her a bit. But the poor toys were really shut up again, and their holiday ended much quicker than they had expected. They heard the distant sounds of the workmen all over the house, and even heard them come into the nursery itself, but they saw nothing more. They could even hear the regular dabs and sweeps of the painter's brush, especially when he was at work on the door that shut them up so closely, and then afterwards they heard the paper hangers ripping off the old papers with a rushing noise, and scraping and sizing the walls for the new paper, but they never got out.

Then the next sounds that greeted them, after a long interval, were the voices of Mr. Spenser and old Mrs. Jones. He had come to see how the house looked after the workmen had left, and she was showing him all over it.

" The nursery looks very nice, sir," she said, as she opened the door, " the old dirty paper all gone, and new paint, you can hardly know it again. This here new paper, to my mind, with the trails of roses and jessamy, is the prettiest in the house ! "

" It looks very clean and bright certainly," replied Mr. Spenser, " but why don't you open this door too ? You can't have too much air ! "

" This is only a cupboard, sir," answered Mrs. Jones. " There were a lot of old playthings left here, and I thought them painters might fling 'em about, so I just turned the key, sir, but I'm going to clean it right down to-morrow.

I thought, sir, that may be, the young ladies and gentlemen might be put out if they found all their little things losed. But here's the key, sir, in my pocket, and now they're all off the premises, there's no need to keep it locked up."

" Quite right, Mrs. Jones," said Mr. Spenser, " I'm very glad you had so much thought. I don't know how Nurse came to overlook this cupboard."

" Why, there, she had such a deal to do with packing up all the things, sir," replied Mrs. Jones, " that t'aint to be wondered at, and its all safe enough to my certain knowledge;" and then, after a little fumbling, she unlocked the door, and threw it wide open, disclosing all the heap of old toys huddled up together.

" Well this *is* a queer collection!" said Mr. Spenser, laughing; " a regular museum of antediluvian playthings! Where on earth could they have come from? I don't remember seeing the children with any of these, even any time back! However, shut them up, Mrs. Jones, till the children come home, and then we'll enquire into the matter!"

Again was the door shut, and the Toys consigned once more to quiet and darkness, but this time only the button was turned, and not the key, so they slumbered peacefully enough and with the hope of freedom before them. And next morning if they had not a holiday to themselves, they had at any rate a little fresh air and sunshine. They were all turned out on the floor, while Mrs. Jones brought her pail and scrubbing brush, and gave the cupboard one of her " good cleans," as she called them. And when it was all thoroughly dry, which she had taken care to hasten by setting the windows and doors open, she came back and began to replace the Toys.

" Now I've cleaned the cupboard, I s'pose I'm bound to tidy up the playthings," said she to herself; " anyhow I'll dust 'em a bit."

How they all quaked as they came under her hands, for she did dust them with a vengeance! She rubbed and scrubbed them with an old piece of tea cloth, she tugged asunder the Kite and the Skipping-rope in a lively manner, that ended in the loss of half his long tail and much of his fringe, she shook the dust out of the old Doll, and almost all the little life and bran she had left with it; she mixed up the Tea-things and Marbles in a bowl of cold water, and then dry rubbed them with a hard duster; she bumped the Ball, she flapped the Toy Kitchen, she rubbed down the Rocking Horse till his last leg fell off; in short she cleaned them all, up and down, till they hardly knew whether they were wood or tin! She finished up by arranging them all after her own fancy on the shelf of the cupboard.

"Well really," said she, taking a step backward to survey the general effect, "it looks almost as nice as a toy shop!" And in the pride of her heart at her own work, she left the door ajar, that it might not be lost upon the family. And by-and-bye the housemaid and cook returned from their holiday, and they set to work and unpacked all the furniture out of the lumber room and replaced each article in its proper position. And the carpenter came and nailed down the carpets and put up the curtains, and the work proceeded fast and merrily, for they were all expected home the next evening. So the Toys heard and saw more life around them

than they had done for years, but they were
not able to resume their gossips, for there were
people in and out the whole day; and even by
night they were not alone, for the cook slept in
the room on a hasty-shake down bed, so as to
be able to get every other room settled. And
when the evening came, the arrival of the family
was soon made known by the noisy bustle of
the children and the clatter all over the house.
The mice trembled with fear behind the wains-
cots, and the crickets shrunk back into their
farthest holes, for they understood well enough
that their reign was over for the present. As
for the Toys, they rather rejoiced than otherwise, for they had been in their time used to
human companionship, and after their lonely
captivity, were not sorry to welcome it once
again.

And as for the children, they were boiling
over with wild spirits and merriment at their
return to such a pleasant, bright home. They
rambled all over the house, and held solemn
councils in each room as to the new paper and
paint, and were altogether thoroughly happy.
Their long visit by the seaside had done them

a world of good, for the fresh salt breezes had seemed to send new strength to every fibre of their bodies and rosy colour to their cheeks, although the sun had done his part so well, that they were tanned of a healthy brown as well as red. Indeed, as Frank said, they had all had a coat of paint too, only that it was of a light mahogany colour!

When Miss Watson came next morning, she was so hugged, and welcomed, and talked to eagerly by all three at once, that after enduring it patiently for a little while, she laughed gaily, and said :—

" My dears, I really must say to you, as the French king did to his courtiers and the donkey, when they all deafened him with their clamour, ' one at a time, gentlemen, if you please!' for while Celia prattles in one ear, and Florry gabbles in the other, and while Frank dances before me and shouts into both, I am quite unable to understand one word from either. You are not more rejoiced to see me than I am to welcome you all back, especially my dear Celia," said Miss Watson, as she affectionately drew Celia close to her and kissed her, " for I see I have been a true prophet, and that you have found the roses I promised you. So I think, as this morning evidently is not likely to be spent in lessons, I must take you one at a time and hear all you have to tell me, only remember, gentlemen, it must be one at a time!"

They all laughed heartily, and promised to comply with her desire, and so, as Frank said he could not keep his word if he stayed there, for he should be sure to begin telling her some of his adventures, he went off to the garden to see how that was getting on, and whether the scarlet runners in his little plot bid fair to give him one dish of beans that year. Florry was so eager to talk to Miss Watson, and so full of chatter, that by common consent she was banished to the nursery, where she made a descent upon the open toy cupboard, and routed them all about till they hardly knew what had come upon them. Meanwhile Miss Watson and Celia had a very pleasant chat upon all that had happened during the holidays. And presently Mrs. Spenser came in, and greeted Miss Watson heartily.

"It does seem so good to be at home

again," she said. "We have enjoyed our trip immensely, and the young folks have benefited by it so much that I quite rejoice in it. Don't you think Celia is looking blooming again, Miss Watson. You were quite right in your predictions; the nice rambles and drives on the beach, and a fair amount of sea bathing, have indeed brought back her rosy cheeks. And Frank is all the better for it too, so I think the change will quite set him up before he goes to Westminster. And I don't know whether they told you that dear Harry came to us from Winchester, and was with us the whole time, which was a great treat, especially to me; and, dear boy, he enjoyed it so much. He is grown such a fine fellow, Miss Watson, you would hardly know your old pupil, and he is now gone to spend the rest of his vacation with his uncle Henry, in the Isle of Man."

"I am sure it has done you all good," replied Miss Watson, "but I must confess, my dear Mrs. Spenser, the change for the better in yourself seems to me the best of all. You were looking so worn and thin when I last saw you, that I observed to my sister I thought *you* were the person who needed change most!"

"I believe I did," answered Mrs. Spenser, smiling; "I had been feeling far from strong for a long while, so that the rest and freedom from care has been a real holiday to me. But I *am* so glad to get home once more, .   .ed, I believe one of the great blessings . going away lies in the pleasure of coming back; and all looks so fresh and bright, it is like a new house!"

"Mamma, Mamma," cried Florry, eagerly, "we have found all the old toys we thought we had lost! There was a cupboard in the nursery, which Nurse says she had lost the key of for a long while—and she thought it was empty. Do come and see, Celia; there's your old doll, and the skipping-rope, and all Harry's marbles, besides the big kite, and such a lot of things. Oh!" said Celia, clapping her hands and dancing round the room, "it's like Ali Baba's hoard of riches, and Frank says it's a regular treasure of Toys!"

WERTHEIMER, LEA AND CO., PRINTERS, FINSBURY CIRCUS.

www.ingramcontent.com/pod-product-compliance
Lightning Source LLC
Chambersburg PA
CBHW030109030726
47498CB00007B/2309